by the same author

Non-Fiction:
GROOVY BOB: THE LIFE AND TIMES OF ROBERT FRASER

HARRIET VYNER

Among Ruins

faber and faber

First published in 2006
by Faber and Faber Limited
3 Queen Square London WC1N 3AU

Typeset by Faber and Faber Limited
Printed in England by Mackays of Chatham plc, Chatham, Kent

A CIP record for this book
is available from the British Library

ISBN 0–571–22592–6

2 4 6 8 10 9 7 5 3 1

To Margaret Vyner

'Men moralise among ruins'
Benjamin Disraeli

PART I

Chapter One

Being lazy, timid and English, Charles Compson had thought that marriage to the unobtainable beauty with whom he was in love, would grant him automatic membership of the easily successful, that he would join the ranks of those who no longer had to try. And indeed, over the subtle congratulatory acclaim, had at once come the deafening winner's clash of yellow coins and treasure – pouring into an unmanageable mountain beside this fulfilled aspiration, the one great success in his life so far. But now this initially gleaming pile, never quite as big as desired, was slithering away at an alarming rate. Its speed of disappearance was almost as great as the changes that would have to take effect should it not reach its original height – or higher, above the visible skies, so that the forays into it might not be noticed.

He always drove fast on the road north as if in urgent haste, and the children's feuds and occasional requests had no effect on the speed.

'Oh, *please!*'

Martin hung his fingers over the back of the driving seat.

'Just, you know, the frog –'

'Sit back! I can't see properly. All right.'

Charles's earliest anecdotal memory was of having come across a huge black growth in the sand by the first of the lakes on his parents' land. Already on an adventure he had persuaded himself to bend down to touch it, but at the moment of tentative contact, it had sprouted bloated dark limbs and hauled itself towards the water with the ungainly movements of a spastic. He had almost been sick, had not dared to run in case chased, but had walked quickly back to the public path that led home.

3

Though unwilling to explore the meaning during the telling, he had at the time put this transfiguration down to a manifestation of justice. He had been out alone in the park without permission and the sort of retribution that would be bound to follow would have no need of the laws of nature.

The children liked the story and always asked for it at some point during the car journey to Northumberland, so as to try again to fish out the ghostly and moral aspects hovering within it. It was this, the repetitive nature of their amusement that Charles's wife, Vivienne, found most annoying. She had no interest in the supernatural, or for that matter the natural; she was bored by both.

'Had it come *out* of the ground?'

'No.'

'Were you scared?'

'Yes.'

'You were the same age as me?'

'About that.'

Vivienne sat unmoving at his side. Sensing her disapproval, Charles gave her knee a clumsy pat.

'What's your earliest memory, then?'

'I haven't got any.'

But she did give a little laugh. She was proud of her own dogged traditionalism, which amused no one but herself; she had always made a point of saying that nothing of her childhood could be of interest to herself or others.

Charles noticed Laura's eyes in the driving mirror.

'Why don't you tell us yours, then?'

But her eyes fell out of sight of their vigil in the mirror.

'I haven't got any either.'

She turned and gave Martin a significant look. He responded immediately. With shrill enthusiasm, he struggled up and launched into a disjointed tale of a ghost with red eyes and just so tall that there was – he thrust forward an inch between finger and thumb – that much between him and the sky . . . By the punch line, a marvel of banal originality, they had swept to a halt in front of the elegant main gates, half hidden by a bend in the road.

Chapter Two

Laura, walking at a more sensible pace, watched Martin running along the corridors like a train, touching each picture as he passed it. More often than not, he was part of the nursery during the school holidays and being neither guest nor family, he was spoilt. His father, Mark, a foreign correspondent, had been at university with Charles, and his mother, Anne, was Charles's oldest friend and neighbour. Constantly travelling, they were grateful for the assurances that Martin's presence was welcome company for Laura.

Now, as was his habit on arrival, he rushed up to the birdcage containing Nanny Hart's budgie Bobby and artfully began to coo through the bars, asking shrilly his usual whimsical questions as to its habits.

'Come on now!'

He took two giant's bounds to the table, then wriggled into his chair.

'Clean?'

Nanny Hart took Laura's other hand and opened it. Inside was a blue pencil.

Laura blushed.

'It's for you.'

'It's not much use to me.'

She put it on the table and turned to Martin. He crammed the toast into his mouth in two huge bites.

'A giant would eat Bobby just like that!'

She took the remains of the toast out of his hand, didn't comment on his laughter.

'So you obviously liked the last dancing class.'

'No – I hated it!'

'It's an early night for you, my boy.'

His attendance at these dancing classes with the royal children had given his presence in the nursery the final seal of acceptance. When Miss Hart accompanied the two of them to these lessons, as she had done the previous week, her eyes remained on the unwieldy stumping boy, enchanted to find himself a giant. If her glance did drift towards the girls' section of the ballroom, Laura's eyes would often be agonisingly turned towards hers or deliberately away, blushing as she continued on tripping with oafish exertion in her fairy rounds.

Miss Hart was a stern woman and disliked the unorthodox. No one could have accused her of hypocrisy; she was quite universal in her systems. Her own lesbianism was squeezed into such tight suppression that it only occasionally had to burst out into gross sentimentality. Her more acceptable alcoholism was indulged in consistent polite secrecy; if it intruded into nursery life at all, it was hidden underneath the covering form of neglect. After dark there was very little the children could do that would draw attention to transgressions of any sort. However, her authority still held during this time and even her occasional maudlin outpourings encouraged no outbreaks of naughtiness. They would play together quietly, knowing when it was time to stop and her good night attentions would have all the distant regret of history.

'She's very pretty! Is that her younger brother?'

'No, but he's my little angel.'

In a few soft words (she had the necessary shorthand of the dancing class audience down to a fine art) Miss Hart had explained to this new nanny, the relationship of the two children, reiterating her preference. And indeed, for those who liked that sort of thing, Martin's animated face was more attractive than Laura's set expression. Her face had been screwed up and guarded like a monkey's and had the same narrow outlines. Even her overabundant curls seemed a mismanaged attempt to bestow sweetness on an unsympathetic site, bouncing uneasily in the pursuit of her aggressive impulses, now curtailed in this ornate room.

'Oh well, it must be nice to have them, friends together.'

And the pleasantry of Martin's presence being a blessing was constantly echoed between the families but, in reality, Laura and he were neither friends nor enemies, but just unconsciously now part of each other's landscape. Occasionally she looked forward to the moment of his arrival, since she had things to tell him and occasionally he responded enthusiastically to such secrets.

And that morning to his parents over breakfast, he had babbled so many anticipatory plans for the puppy that had been promised, that Anne had confessed to the Compsons as she dropped him off in time for the journey north, of being a little jealous of his evident preference of home.

Chapter Three

The library curtains fell voluptuously, like the dresses of female saints, patterned and glorious. Having once or twice visited his London home in the old days, Charles's country house was smaller than Freddie had envisioned, but its interiors were splendid indeed. Recently Freddie had spent some considerable time wandering around the National Gallery. Although British painters were in a minority, the English having always been stronger in appreciation than application, it was a collection that represented all that the nation had chosen over the years. Thus surely it would provide some clues towards the national psyche? But really, in his dignified stroll around the seventeenth- and then eighteenth-century rooms, his mind was full of the dismal finality of his own story having finished.

His first expulsion from Africa, thirteen years earlier, after a bloodless and temporarily successful coup on the British governor general's part, had brought him attention and acclaim back in England. Dinners had been given for him and invitations issued to his Eaton Square apartment. Now, thirteen years later, on this second exile, his more dramatic stories of death and battle soon seemed to pall, though on his first few months of arrival, this had pleased him, suggesting that he had been correct in thinking that the English had got their priorities right.

One literary friend had had a sudden frantic enthusiasm on listening to his tales, and had insisted that he should produce in biographical form a sort of African Odyssey of betrayal and fortitude. He had arranged for him to have lunch with a representative of a well-known publishing house. Even this man, so professional in his attentions, had fallen finally into a kind of weariness. At first, with discriminating smiles, he had interjected his enthusiasm for the project, in between

9

Freddie's laconic but unceasing descriptions of betrayal and narrow squeaks on the bloody road away from the besieged Mengo Hill Palace. But by the end of the second course, he was glancing at his watch; his voice had dropped at least an octave from its initially excited pitch.

His book had recently been published, and a party given for its launch by the same literary friend who had initiated its creation. It had been a friendly gathering but hardly luminous. The book had then, over the course of the next two months, received two short but respectful reviews from Africa-loving journalists. They had not been able to resist putting in their own versions of the events described, but both had come up with the commendation 'unique' when referring back to his.

'I'll put it here, next to another favourite.'

Charles had seemed genuinely to appreciate the book, which Freddie had signed for him, 'to afternoons with friends'. He pulled out *Eminent Victorians* so as to place Freddie's next to it.

'A valued part of my library!'

Now Freddie was drunk. Lying back on the sofa complacently, he continued his meandering perusal of the room. He was glad that Edward had persuaded him into the visit, having described Charles's Northumberland property as 'enchanting', enunciated in that special way that Freddie took to mean 'Not commensurate with my own'. And the house was by no means as grand as Edward's, being considerably smaller, but it had dignity. He looked out of the windows at the wild weather. Black crows were being pushed upwards and backwards by the wind in exuberant abandonment to superior elements.

'Hooray!'

The door had opened and the children were coming in tentatively, but giggling at Edward Kielder's raised arms and greeting. Charles was out of the room and Vivienne's manner turned brisk and almost panicky.

'Children, this is Lord and Lady Kielder – you've met before haven't you? And this is King Freddie – Martin and Laura.'

'Hello. Hello.'

The children's eyes slid away as soon as they'd completed their greeting. The titles presented so abruptly had put them off and the King was black.

'Where has Charles gone?'

Vivienne had no enthusiasm for the forthcoming puppy ceremony, but she felt it unfair that she was to have to bear its burden.

'Oh, Vivienne – he was going to find a record we'd talked about.'

And as Charles made his returning entrance, the notes of this favourite song just preceded him.

Freddie circled his hand in gratitude, singing along when possible in a high soft voice:

> '. . . If I were a catfish
> Swimming in the deep blue sea
> I'd have all you women
> Diving after me . . .'

Nanny Hart always made her opinion quite clear and the children too had their own little joke concerning this particular song heard distantly and so often up on the nursery floor. Now they laughed together, with little attempt at their usual concealment.

Charles ignored them, and asked Edward, 'Good, isn't it?'

He attempted to snap his fingers to the rhythm.

'Oh, very lovely! Such a funny and sad little song! Lead-belly – what do you think children?'

They quite liked Lord Kielder (now even to them, his title seemed an appropriate excuse for his eccentricity, and so no mouthful to use), and his kindly smile, an anarchic gleam behind it, brought out their cruelty.

'Lovely –!'

They laughed further as the song built to a mournful climax.

'– trum*pet*!'

They screwed up their faces disgustedly, clapped their hands to their ears in a paroxysm of exhibitionism.

'Not trumpet. Harmonica.'

There was a tap at the door and the room fell silent.

'Come in.'

The children, having heard the sullen nature of Charles's correction, were subdued suddenly. Superstitiously, they feared that their rude high spirits might have ruined the occasion altogether. And when the door inched open with suitable drama, revealing at its base a brown terrier face (a hand just visible behind it, urging it into the room) they hardly dared to be too appreciative of the moment.

After initial interest – even the sulky Charles could not resist the lure of the puppy – the adults went back to their conversation. But suddenly Freddie slid down towards the children. The little dog, surprised, gave two disconcerted yaps in his direction. It was awkward having him down there, sprawled out elegantly on the floor. He snapped his fingers in comical timing. The puppy at last decided to enjoy the humour of the gesture and pounced. They all laughed and Laura grabbed the puppy, asking, 'Do you have any dogs?'

'I used to have two pet bears at my palace.'

The children stared at him suspiciously.

'What were they called?'

'Hymn and Honey.'

He leant towards the puppy, and growled, 'And they would have eaten *you* – *right up*!'

'No.'

Laura got up and raised her arms.

'No. He would have grabbed them and –'

Her wrestling movements caught Vivienne's eye and she called Freddie over with apologies. As they walked, he referred back to his time on the floor.

'What delightful children; so pretty, your daughter.'

'Rather showing off at the moment, I'm afraid.'

Freddie demurred politely. He imagined English disinge-
nuity in her clipped reply. But Laura was at that moment
mauling round the dog in rather too much of a winsome way
for Vivienne's liking. Looking at her face, surrounded by
dark curls, pressed against the dog's head, looking up
towards them from time to time, her artfulness struck an irritating note.

After the birth of Laura, Vivienne had gaily confounded
those who might have expected the desire for a son, with her
satisfaction in having produced this daughter. With tones of
authority, she had insisted that both she and Charles had
wanted a girl, and she had believed it of herself certainly.
Perhaps there had been some thought of the burden that
would have ensued from the birth of a son. But she had
brushed over too lightly the prospect of an echo of her
younger self.

From her hospital bed, she had decided on the name over
Charles's preferred Elizabeth – her rights of choice were
unassailable. But over the years, complied with on all matters
concerning Laura, her authoritarianism had died down with
her interest.

As she grew up, Laura looked more and more like her
paternal grandfather. But still, a faintly disturbing image had
sprung directly from a time Vivienne would have preferred
gone, and was growing, pushing out and developing in a
similar way to her own. It was a replay she was bound to
have to watch. It felt as inescapable as the dream she had had
that night. In it she had watched Laura and another play and
argue in an orchard. It had been all too prettily reminiscent
of those Victorian paintings, filled with blossoms and dire
warnings of punishments about to descend for transgressions
that would seem in modern times to be inoffensive.

'Now, are you music lovers accompanying us on our walk?'

'Yes, they are.'

13

Charles's curt tones accurately reflected his deflation, his remaining irritation at the children's priggish conservatism of taste. He was even irritated at Edward's invitation. He would have preferred that they be left behind.

Chapter Four

Martin was not good with the dog, anyone could see that, but to Charles's dissatisfaction and relief, his failure in coercing him into his violent games was causing him to lose interest and veer off down the grass banks alone, arms outstretched. Charles answered Edward's enquiry courteously.

'Yes, I *believe* so, that's what they say – just under the main structure of the presbytery itself.'

As they walked, Edward touched on several local legends in his dry manner. He alluded to the apocryphal but charming tale of the saint, once a soldier of King Edwin, who had been about to kill one of the divinely protected wild pigs milling about on the holy spot, driven to this sacrilege by love of the hunt. A vision of the divine benefactress had stayed his hand and transformed his life to one of prayer. It was on this spot, formally a pagan sanctuary, from which had sprung the much later Christian abbey.

'But you see each region has its own claims, and of course, many of these Northumbrian legends echo others from further south.'

Edward Kielder brought with him an atmosphere of calm, even now apparent in the face of his increasing enthusiasm as their journey brought them nearer to the ancient monument and the purported burial site. Indeed, his serenity would have been an endorsement for his philosophy had it not been for the exaggerated nature of its premise. Freddie listened to his friends' talk about saints and kings. He was not introspective, but he was a drunkard and so was sentimental, furiously so. This walk down perfectly acceptable tracks, under trees he could perfectly well have managed to negotiate, turned his thoughts sour with the remembrance of all he had lost.

'. . . originally buried near the cave that had been his place of contemplation, his bones were reputedly returned by his followers, lain in a makeshift burial chamber – the site from which the abbey rose some five centuries later.'

They walked on in silence for a while. Edward had had many strange experiences and had come to firm conclusions, unshaken by his own sense of humour and that of others. His historical scholarship was respected but his interests having expanded into the esoteric, he was quite prepared to keep to himself the enjoyment of his newer beliefs. To scrape beneath the visible picture of the present, as he had oftentimes done, was to witness the living ancestral originals, spiralling back even to the point of this planet's life, initiated by wiser beings. But he knew how his theories, constructed painstakingly from dreams, visions and visitations were perceived by those outside his scheme of things; by, in fact, the whole of the world.

Having passed the first of the lakes, they now were under the shadows of the trees that lined the path leading up to the little temple folly above. For these few paces, their eyes had rest from the excesses of beauty. Having followed the same route as today's, it had been at this same spot a little over ten years ago, that Charles had asked Vivienne to marry him. Instinctively he had felt that its modesty was appropriate for this delicate question, although sentimentally, he had been proud to show her the magnificence of the rest of the grounds. The memory of that time filled his heart now with some sort of twilight melancholy, which seemed almost more in line with the surroundings.

Having asked the question, which in his heart he had no thought that she would refuse, he had walked alongside her till round the corner, the ruins of the abbey had been revealed again, the river behind them and the formality of the next lakes just glimpsed. The sun had come out and the stones had lit up in a trumpet blast of celestial encouragement. In the clipped and jokey way she had, she had taken Charles's hand

and given it a momentary squeeze in that picturesque moment of radiance.

'I think that would be very nice.'

Charles could not altogether call himself a nature lover since he was almost more drawn to the man-made than the natural in terms of aesthetics and pleasure. For example, almost certainly it had been Vivienne's consummate artificiality of manner as much as her beautiful face that had struck such a tremendous chord. Whether this chord had been one of familiarity or novelty he couldn't have said. Perhaps, had he been pushed, he might have concluded that certain of the elements were familiar enough to allow him to take the alien ones into his timid hands and leap forward with them into a precariously novel future.

'This needs some restorative work.'

They climbed up the track to the little Temple of Galatea. Behind the Doric columns was a small reluctant window allowing the viewer a distant glimpse of the sea. The hard work was still left for them to do.

'This is England at its best!'

Freddie's voice was filled with restrained compassion, the result of training accorded to all royalty, who had to have their own courtier-like tact. With mournful appreciation, he was concluding that the park was beautiful indeed, but it lacked the robust vivacity of his lost Bugandan kingdom. Kingdom. He repeated the word again with the sentimental provocation of a drunkard, nudging himself crassly towards greater self-pity. The estate obviously was the apotheosis of the English idea of beauty. But he was just a little sick of English subtlety, so much hankered after over the years.

Freddie had once admired the unsaid, the undone, the polite English disregard of the disagreeable. His short education in England at an impressionable age had given him a thrilling taste of the poetry in these silences. But now, since he was a victim of these very attributes, he was beginning to see these neglectful gaps, not as potential riches but as the voids of

17

infinite space between the visible stars. No meaning, nothing there but stardust, the balls of dust under a rented London bed.

'Oops! All right? A bit steep.'

They inched themselves down the track and walked on. And finally ahead of them, the light on the abbey's venerable tower masonry twinkled in echoed reflection on the blue surface of the lake. Even the most commanding of the visitors had let slip expressions of sentimentality at moments like these but Charles had been able to erect a barrier between himself and that small proportion of his mind and soul that would expand in understanding of the meaning of beauty.

The estate had been passed on to Charles eighteen years ago. His father, with his usual brisk disregard for lengthy deliberation, had heeded the tax advice, and now he and Charles's mother, Edith, lived in Scotland. He visited occasionally and Charles would walk round the grounds with him, explaining his timetable for the tasks ahead. In the presence of his father, Charles found it hard to be articulate or persuasive and the walks were always frustrating. However, during the years that it had belonged to him, Charles had found that he had an eye for the landscaping vision necessary for such an estate, and his pleasure and exactitude during the solitary walks might have surprised those who found him vague.

The grounds were open to the public and now they stepped aside, holding back a sycamore branch to allow a couple easier access to the steep path. It gave Charles pleasure that the place was enjoyed but it was one of his weaknesses that the additional tax advantages proposed rendered him timid and dreamy. Now, as they continued on down, he was able to outline some of his landscaping and restorative plans in quite dispassionate manner; he felt at that moment quite able to brush aside his financial fears as being superstitious and likely to amount to nothing.

Charles had always been fatalistic to the point of lunacy,

but it was an attitude that, had he known about it, Freddie could have sympathised with. They had both built admirable buttress walls to prevent the armies of the past from performing their acts of abundant cruelty. The constituents of these armies may have been pitifully inadequate but pitted together en masse, in unceasing campaigning obstinacy, they could overcome any attempts to laugh them into retreat. And of course, these shadowy workers were carrying out their unceasing forays behind the ramparts even now. Their sightless and soundless presence could be felt, even before their work would create a chink or two in the walls, which by this method were doomed, of course, to fall in time.

And as they walked on, the abbey spread itself out fully, ruined and gracefully captured. It was impossible to tell what made the sight so magnificent; it seemed that all the ingredients, both man-made and natural had come together not so much in harmony (which would have been depressingly suburban) but in severity. But to neither of the observers at that moment did the whole reflect the usual harshness and overwhelming infinity of the Almighty. This impression could be left to others, allowed to give full rein to romantic impulses. Terror at the hint of God (if they so believed) and the poignancy of perfection apparently observing them coolly with the absolute detachment of a creator.

'Charles?'

'Oh, yes, thank you.'

Having lit their cigarettes with difficulty in the wind, they remained for a while watching Edward pottering around with his measuring equipment some way ahead. Finally, extinguishing his cigarette under his foot, Charles walked casually towards the children, who were noisily attempting to persuade the puppy to take advantage of the splendid amenities of this large estate, now his. The woods, lakes and other dogs belonging to the many sightseers, they were pointing out to him with gestures of encouragement, were there for the taking. But he seemed reluctant to indulge in the joys of this sort of freedom, following them in fits and starts or lying down bashfully. Charles sat gingerly on one of the mossy stones of the refectory and watched them.

They circled round again and ended up beside Edward. He stood up from his examinations patiently, apparently explaining something to them, gesturing as he did so. From where Charles could see them, it appeared that the children had assumed the position of suspicious avidity. They stood at his side, their faces frozen to his, following the directions of his pointing fingers with reluctance, fascinated but disbelieving. Then they wheeled off again, and left him to his studies.

Finally the whole party set off home. The children wanted to show off their mastery, but the puppy still stuck to them, lay down or wheedled round them, overwhelmed by so much space, and if occasionally interested in a leaf or two, soon ran back to their feet again. He would not obey their command to hunt.

'Go on, puppy! Go on!'

'Leave him alone now, he's had enough.'

At those words the puppy lay down with a look of suffering.

'Shall I pick him up?'

'Just leave him, he'll catch up.'

But this prediction proved inaccurate and soon the children, anguished by the diminishing sight behind them, appealed mutely to Charles. They knew he liked dogs, he had had one as a child who bit everyone but him. There was a pause as he prepared to put his powers once again to the test. He bent down, looking in the direction of the distant animal.

'Come on – Puppy – come here.'

He had a kind voice. The dog wagged his tail and moved as if to get up, but slumped apologetically.

'Come here!'

And suddenly he rose and ran towards them, cringing at their feet with their jubilation. The children then ran on ahead, calling him, and miraculously he followed them in a slow series of lurching bounds.

Charles lay on top of his bed early that evening, in a pleasant mood in spite of the deadened grogginess of having just slept. He had rather liked the afternoon; not only for the company, which had been amenability itself, but the effect his own contributed bits and pieces of local lore had had on the nodding and scribbling Edward. And the little taste of the occult too, like a paddle at the seaside, had calmed his nerves. These waves dribbling pleasantly over his feet and receding, had left an agreeable memory and only a suggestion of man's mysterious beginnings, hidden along with its unseen inhabitants, the creatures as unsightly as rubbish sacks within its dark depths.

Of course, it could only be saints or lunatics, having sensed this particular fragment of the universe, who would throw over everything to pursue its invisible trails. Who else but these could pursue such a whimsical mission in the midst of the mental nagging of habitual priorities of modern life to re-assert themselves?

Nevertheless, Charles felt that he had retained something from the afternoon, perhaps flattered into belief by the absolute authority granted him by ownership. It was as if, in an absurd attempt at dressing up, a cloak had been gravely placed around his shoulders – and now, he couldn't avoid it, he did indeed feel in some way imbued with the holy spirit of this mythical and charming patron saint of swine.

Chapter Five

The colours in the bar were all dark greens and browns, suggesting the smoking or billiard room of a grand house. The owner, Julian Anthony, had used his limited aristocratic education to good effect, mixing the grotesque and familiar in a style so beloved of the sorts of clients he had succeeded in establishing as regulars. Not the least of these lures was his mother, Joan, attractive also to the younger generation of artists for her rubbery features and repulsively familiar manner. Most nights, she sat on the green chair in the hall with her legs resolutely apart, rising heavily to collect the coats of more favoured clients, hurling them at the cloakroom girl as she swapped coarse asides with their owners.

Charles stood for a while in the entrance hall, snapping his finger joints but otherwise responding to her intrusions humorously. She had made it her business to include him in her inner circles, his losses and insouciance in the face of loss having all the hallmarks of grandeur. He was not titled but, of course, his Northumberland estate was famous all over England. Now he looked a little bashful, and had an unknown client witnessed their one-sided badinage, they would have wondered at her persistence and, perhaps, judgement. She nudged him.

'In a winning mood?'

'I hope so.'

She leant her face close to his confidentially. 'You fucking *show* him; my son's a greedy bugger!'

He smiled, blushing.

'I hope to do just that . . .'

She stood back speculatively.

'Don't hope, dear. *Do* it!'

The trace of sorrow in her voice was a recognised addition to the grotesque joke that she embodied. Her repulsive qualities never palled to these observers – since childhood they had been inclined towards the repetitive cruel silliness engendered by public school fatalism. But as it had been pointed out by cooler observers, it was just these old school ties, were he poetically inclined, that Julian might have pictured, flung round the necks of these young men and pulled on with gentle force until they inched step by step into his rooms.

Charles entered the first room timidly, but at once was greeted by a man who had been sitting in one of the armchairs, observing the play on a nearby table.

'A drink?'

'I think I will. Whisky.'

'Do you intend to make a night of it?'

Charles could neither remember this man's name, nor his form, but answered with a smile of scrupulous courtesy.

'If it works out that way.'

'Blackjack I suppose?'

'No, I thought roulette.'

'Oh – leaving your chances to fate?'

'That's right.'

As they waited for the drinks, Charles began to feel impatient. Memories, the embarrassing encounter with the bank manager that week, who had interrupted Charles's anecdote ('I think, if we may, we must return to the matter at hand . . . ') kept taking root and the only acting antidote was being withheld by this call for courtesy. Always, the moment Charles picked up his chips to begin play, the perpetual hour by hour anxieties, that seemed in daily life to consume him with their feeble graspings, were crushed, obliterated into darkness by the intriguing momentum.

Finally he heard the words: 'Well. Good luck.'

'Thank you.'

And the man got up and moved away to another table with desultory interest, leaning slightly towards the action, but from a polite distance. There hardly seemed any point to his being in the place.

Charles squinted at his watch in the street light – it was five o'clock in the morning. He had left the club on his own, which is what he wished. His friend Richard had offered to accompany him to another club or back home, but Charles felt only the desire for solitude.

It had recently been raining, violently apparently. Although he was drunk, nevertheless Charles was profoundly happy. Up until that moment (although he hadn't realised it) he had been in a state of agitation, lured towards the sirens' songs of possibilities ahead. All that week their wings had been fluttering above his head, invisibly, but he had felt them and listened to their suggestions of what could be done, this and that, in the expansion of the future that victory would bring. Their disappearance had been as dramatic as a puff of smoke with the last chips taken.

There had been slow looks and movements away from the bystanders or sometime players, an atmosphere of studied casualness. But then the only other player present with a similar propensity for recklessness had unexpectedly placed his hand on his back, given it a light tap. This man, Christopher Kovel, was not usually given to camaraderie; his discourtesy was as notorious as his indelicate artistry. Charles had blushed and smiled, had received a bow in return that had seemed to be without the usual traces of irony to be found in such a gesture.

Charles thought back briefly to his subsequent chat about future arrangements with the affable Julian, who had seemed to think that grace in victory lay in rubbing the situation's most dramatic aspects in Charles's face, perhaps as if crediting him with absolute courage in defeat. Charles's need to match this expectation halfway gave his solitude now some considerable compensatory ease.

Curzon Street was cold and the lights were shining prettily

in the wet pavements. He looked down at his black shoes, one after the other swishing through the pools of shallow water. The water seeping now through his shoes seemed intriguing. He was happy; were he not married, he'd have been happy for ever, but still . . .

Charles stood for a moment at the corner of Clarges Street and contemplated whether to walk further. He felt a little ashamed suddenly of walking at this hour of the morning, but as the consideration breezed through his mind, a sudden freedom marched him on towards Green Park. Weaving along the paths there, through the correct trees so representative of their unquestioning era, he felt in his feet the looming prospect of future conversations.

Perhaps Julian's gladiator assumptions concerning Charles's defeat had been correct, since his next instinct was to head for his club for breakfast, in order that he might not wake anyone in the house. The trials of having to revert back to putting a brave face on the interesting events of the evening seemed if anything to speed up his stubborn pace.

It was not that he had ever inspired envy in his contemporaries, his chagrined response to good fortune gave rise in the spectators to speculative reappraisal of the gifts landing at his feet; the property made over to him at a young age, his marriage. But if then, no gloating, there would be at least great curiosity, since the calamitous news and the shock waves of its inevitable consequences must surely have floated instinctively and speedily through the vacuous early morning to the one place with ears alert to hear it.

Walking past the Ritz, a familiar doorman was looking dismally out, rubbing his hands against the cold. There were no guests around at this hour and he could drop his formality. He had sacrificed the more demanding and civilised hours to the younger members of staff who had families.

Charles knew him from over ten years back. He had become part of their then weekly ritual, in which Charles and his mother, Edith, would indulge in an afternoon tea next to the gold fish fountains, progressing if the mood took them (and it always did) on to the first dry Martini of the evening. Part of their unassuming pleasure lay in the quirks of the other patrons and more affectionately, in the enthusiasm of this doorman's greetings at the hotel entrance. Stubbornly preventing their progress for some minutes, he would find respectful allusions to Edith's distant family members and throw in his own connections, cousins who were part of the staff at other ancestral houses. He would vibrate in his quest to reveal her illustrious antecedents, unknown to other members of the hotel staff, and sometimes to Edith herself, his exploratory net was flung so wide. The fierce nostalgia in his eyes always rather startled Edith, who had never known this ardent thrill of snobbery. In her timid mind, the variations of rank had their place, but passion was an alien eccentricity.

Now Charles gave him a smile and he barely responded, until suddenly his mouth opened in an O of recognition. In a gesture of unexpected and not especially friendly frivolity, he tipped his top hat slightly in a jaunty salute.

As he walked on, Charles found himself somewhat disconcerted by this greeting. Its meaning dug around his mind. Either the doorman had mistaken him for another regular or – his status had fallen in the intervening hour in between leaving the club and his walking past the hotel.

Chapter Six

Charles's father, Hilary, had no time for the sort of art on the walls of his son's house. Established masterpieces he respected, but too much interest even in their direction he would have understood as being indications of sentimentality. But works from those days were decorative and portraits were informative. The paintings hanging on the walls of Charles's London house were deliberately hideous, as if setting down some sort of irritating challenge to those like himself who disliked the destruction of perfectly good traditions, and had no interest in engagement.

He kept his face impassive but his blue eyes remained fixed on the paintings on the wall beside the door, a downwards pointing triangle with a dot in its middle and the next – a snake? He supposed them to have been expensive. He had once asked the price of one new purchase and had not known whether the blaze in his son's eyes was of defiance or triumph at his exclamation of disbelief.

He leant towards Edith and said with a nod towards them. 'New?'

'I think so.'

He supposed them to have something to do with Vivienne's influence, but at once his impatience left him and he felt something like amusement.

He and Edith had disliked the idea of Vivienne when first her name began to be placed, with small but significant emphasis, into Charles's anecdotes. They had imagined vulgarity. Again, Hilary had suspected Charles to be branching out into new and unsuitable areas for his own stubborn reasons.

But at their first meeting they had been won over almost from the moment she had swept into the room with grave welcome, looking startlingly elegant and talking about their recent trip to Paris. Being their first encounter with this sort of manufactured charm, it had immobilised them, rendered them docile to a fault. And having met his match, Hilary remained frightened of her a little. Such feelings were a novelty and he didn't recognise the little traces of fear present. Instead, having succumbed totally, he now looked forward to their meetings, at which his views would be challenged most stimulatingly and amusingly.

Edith still had her very faint doubts, though perhaps doubts would be too strong a word since her feelings were so wordless and unformed. These sorts of misgivings applied in faded fashion to every area of her life. Vivienne's spell she felt to be a little invasive but she admired her.

They had been waiting for her arrival and a snatch of clipped conversation outside the door preceded her entrance with Charles into the sitting-room. Vivienne did not look beautiful at that moment, her mouth was pulled down and her eyes were fractious. She greeted them with her usual energy but then sat herself down with unusual silence, her arms folded.

Charles began to talk and as she heard the information being stubbornly presented, Edith began to feel a rare emotion and that was anger. If she had not had faith in his actual abilities, then she had had faith in his future. She had recognised his vulnerability from an early age, had trained herself to appreciate it. His older brother, David, having been killed a week before the outbreak of war in a doomed night flight exercise that even his reckless ingenuity was unable to circumnavigate, soon after Edith had shifted her loyalty to the more feminine Charles. She had persuaded herself that his delicacy was as admirable in its way as David's robust heroism. And over the twenty or so years that had followed, her private faith in Charles's worth had grown in proportion to the disbelief that characterised Hilary's reaction to Charles's increasingly wild and modern schemes. As she listened, she would hold to herself the faith that something greater than her husband's logical objections would prevail in the matter of Charles's increasing whimsicality of lifestyle.

Now, nothing of her disappointment was revealed, even as the information grew increasingly grim, delivered in faltering but defiant bursts. All things then considered, the estate would have to go. It was impractical even to think of selling off parts of it. He had already had talks with representatives of the local Northumbrian council and the British Heritage Trust. Edith refused to give in to the morbid impulse to look to her husband. Happily she found that an imperceptible movement of her eyes sufficed, since his flickering face was reflected in the mirror beside the fireplace. As she might have expected, he sat impassive, his hands clasped comfortably, the grim and absorbed expression of one listening to a radio play. He was triumphant! His son, having been handed the box of matches, had set himself ablaze and their own house with it. All those clues suggesting that mishandling of finances, slapdash accounting and worse, had been absolutely accurate, they had steered him towards the absolutely correct conclusion.

Charles had the task of seeing each member of staff separately in order to tell them the news. Their reactions were both stoical and unexpected. Charles explained that since the Kentigern estate's new owners, the British Heritage Trust, wished to maintain the same high standards presently running in the properties and grounds, it had been made clear to him that there would be a place for all those who wished to stay on.

'Thank you.'

'No, thank *you*.'

As he waited for Mrs Ruth the housekeeper, he wondered if he could have arranged for a less formal manner of announcing the news. He played with the paperweight on his desk. It had been in his Christmas stocking. It was a very realistic depiction of an orange, leaf curled under and part of the inside segments showing, yellow veins and all. It was the kind of object that appealed to all of them as a family and he had been surprised when Anne had indicated on Boxing Day that she found it somewhat unattractive. What was there unattractive about it? And his face took on the familiar stubborn look of a man clinging to beliefs about taste. There was a knock and Mrs Ruth came in. Charles stood up, feeling that that was more appropriate, put down the orange and held out his hand.

With one unpleasant experience out of the way Charles couldn't quite understand why he was embarking on another. This corridor he was walking down was one he rarely used and he felt intrusive, tapping on and opening the door behind which were issuing subdued noises of movement and talk.

'Hello!'

And a silence greeted his arrival. The two children stared at him from their colouring in on the floor. But his unexpected presence, appearing shyly in the midst of their toys and games in the nursery, would always induce in both children an immediate intoxication. Now they jumped up and pulled at him to join them on the floor.

'Look! Look – this is my one, she's on a shell that's a boat, look.'

'Oh yes, Greek myths.'

Though touched by their enthusiasm, it contributed to the feeling he always had, of intruding into lives with which he had nothing in common. Sitting down awkwardly in the suit worn for the dismissal procedure, he tried to respond to the explanation that accompanied each drawing.

'Look, the fish –'

With a sly glance, she added, '– the *cat*fish . . .'

'Yes.'

'– is being used as a –'

'As a trumpet – yes, that's right.'

30

He felt as out of place as if, visiting an African village, he had been induced to join the ritual dance of welcome, watched all the time by the authoritative guide. His very confusion encouraged further hilarious cruelty. They began to pull roughly at his sleeve, push him towards one spot then change their minds noisily.

But tonight boredom came to Charles's aid; he extracted himself and turned resolutely towards Miss Hart.

'I'm going for a spot of fishing a bit later this afternoon, Miss Hart, and I was thinking the children might want to come?'

She looked back at him politely.

'Martin is coming down with a cold, but perhaps Laura would like to go?'

'Yes!'

And Laura strode up to him, took his arm and dragged him out of the room. Halfway along the corridor, she paused. Of course he needed an explanation for the hold up.

'Wait . . .'

And then her mind was made up.

'I've just got to do one thing, one thing!'

She signalled to him fiercely, one finger held up, walking fast backwards, towards the nursery again. Going through the door, she pulled off the lucky bracelet on her wrist, a free gift in her comic that week. She approached the disappointed Martin feverously.

'This is for you, to make up for it.'

Martin took the coveted magic bracelet with surprising indifference. He was sat at the table with Miss Hart; both were leaning over his colouring-in.

'He wanted it.'

'Well you better not keep your father waiting.'

'Can I take the dog on just a quick walk?'

Her artful tone was unnecessary, her restlessness had been irritating Charles. She had been standing watching him

31

untangle the line, her offer to help had been declined and for a time she had been asking the usual stream of questions, both pointless and distracting.

'On the beach? Yes, don't be long, and don't let the dog run off.'

'But how can I stop him? Oh, all right.'

The two of them had run along the path, and finally had disappeared over the bank that led to the beach. Charles was able to sort out the tangle finally and was able to start fishing. He cast several times, and at once got a bite. It got away but he looked round to see if Laura was back to witness the near thing. Instead, to his slight dismay he saw the figure of Mr Harding, the under-gardener on the far side of the river, coming down from the woods and on his way back from the abbey, his evening walk. He stopped at a respectful distance, lifting his arm in greeting.

'Almost. Shame!'

'Yes.'

Charles happily kept up the loud stream of agreement to his initial flow of pleasantries. He knew from long experience that Mr Harding's meandering stream of thoughts, though haphazard in origin, would always finish along absolutely familiar and dull routes. It was a family joke picked up even by the children who liked to wriggle with duplicated boredom at his intriguing lore. But today his manner turned peculiarly lively, unpleasantly so. He referred back to the subject of the move to come with more than one spiteful angle of analysis.

Finally he asked, 'Are the children around?'

'No. Just Laura and she's off somewhere. She's taken the dog down to the beach.'

'They'll miss the beaches.'

'I know.'

'So, a spot of fishing anyway?'

'Yes!'

Charles's heartiness at last informed him that perhaps his

uncharacteristic mark had been made. After his goodbyes, he left, walking up towards the homeward path that he had taken earlier, and Charles was able to settle back to solitude.

Perhaps her inability to control the dog had annoyed the man. He was looking at her with a blank look and had stopped what he was doing, but still bent down towards the ground. The sun suddenly appeared and the whole beach was lit up.

She moved closer and then to be polite, asked, 'What are you collecting?'

He didn't answer, just stood up courteously as if it were an effort. Then he held out his hands in which were three shells.

'Pretty.'

'I'm making a picture.'

He returned to his task, one eye on her as she started looking towards the ground.

'These?'

She picked up two and held them up, but he said, 'They have to be pink for the stamen. Do you know what a stamen is? It's the inside of the flower – look.' And the mussel shell did have a pink lining.

'I'll help.'

They worked in silence. After a while she placed her seven shells beside his in the sand and he singled out one.

'Blue, you see, just like a mermaid's tail.'

'Yes.'

'Do you like swimming in the sea too?'

'I can swim now without armbands.'

'That's good. Shall we go swimming then?'

Laura laughed, looking at him cautiously.

'It's too late!'

'Perhaps it is.'

He bent down again.

'But can I see your picture?'

He considered her request shyly.

'See it? Well since you've been such a help – perhaps you should.'

Every other step was a shuffle to keep up with him.

'Where do you live?'

'In a cave under the sea!'

She laughed, then said, 'Wait!'

She took off her coat and put it on the grass, ran to catch up. When they got to the rock pool, he held back, looked out into the distance and she did too, walking forward to dig her toes into the sandy edge. There was no one ahead, except a small moving dot.

She exclaimed in excitement, 'Look, he's there, Peter the dog – I told you –'

And from behind she heard him coming like the wind, and it was too late.

The sea sounded loud, and he was lying some distance away, curled up. Her clothes were off below and she was cold. She inched up her leggings and put her toes into the top of her wellingtons. She pulled at the strange scarf, his. Its cold rendered it slimy, she felt sick to touch it. But it wouldn't come off. The alternative, of leaving it round her neck was not feasible. She sat up and pulled at it with both hands and it came off. She put it on the sand beside the pool. It was purple and had a gold shiny pattern.

There was a movement and he got up. He turned to look at her but said nothing. Her clothes were wet and she picked at the ingrained sand, then stood up. She feared turning, leaving him unseen, as she walked further and further away and towards safety. He stood still, empty and incapable. She held out her hand, said softly testing her voice that pushed uncomfortably against the tight neck of her jumper.

'Shall we go?'

On the way she kept hold of his hand, pulled him at one point – he looked enquiringly and she let go of his hand, picked up her dropped coat and put it on. Her voice was stronger by the minute and she briefly chatted.

He cleared his throat. Finally he said, 'It's best you don't tell anyone.'

'No. I swear on the Bible.'

There was a noise behind them and he jumped.

She turned for him and exclaimed, 'It's only the dog – Peter! Bad dog! Where have you been?'

The three of them walked in silence and then saying good-bye, Laura with Peter headed back up towards Charles's fishing spot.

'I spoke to someone.'

'Did you?'

'He was collecting shells.'

Charles remembered himself, dragging himself from advanced nostalgia.

'You shouldn't speak to strangers.'

'I know.'

The dark cloud rushed over the light scattered stones like a frown. A sudden splat of rain followed, but as an afterthought. It cleared immediately.

'Shall we try a cast or two?'

She nodded and sat on a boulder. She was shivering, but unwilling to return home yet. She obscurely felt that some-thing was waiting for her there – justice. She saw him strug-gling and stood shyly.

'Shall I hold it?'

'Thanks.'

His cigarette obscured his speech, but she held the rod and looked at his concentration, untangling the line.

'Right.'

He cast the fly and she stood discreetly to one side, finger-ing the net that she would use should they be lucky.

'You know.'

He took one last puff and flipped the cigarette into the river.

'We're going to have to move.'

She didn't want to. She was cold and wanted to stay there.

'Where – to over there?'

She pointed hopefully towards the nearby pool that was Charles's usual choice. Its black water glinted with the promise of fish underneath.

'No, I meant.'

He wound in his line and once he had caught the fly, flying through the air wilfully in every direction, he turned to her.

'I meant, we are going to have to move away from here (he waved his hand in a brisk half circle) to another house.'

'Oh.'

It was getting dark, but it was at the grey stage. This warning phase filled her with panic. It was as if night had given them a dare – to get home quick. You have this chance. No chance at all would have been safer.

'Shall we go back now?'

'Yes, I'm packing up.'

They had only a small time and he was being so slow. She walked close to him. And could she trust him to be fearless? Could she rely on him? Doubts and fearful propositions formed fearful unfinished images for every future step.

'But where we're going might be nice.'

A slow apparition rose out of the low water ahead, white arms outstretched and Charles lurched, let out an involuntary 'Oh!'

Then as the bird settled in the water again, he laughed at his own fright and looked back at Laura impassively standing, her eyes frozen on his. His hand was on her arm and he suddenly noticed the condition of her clothes.

'Hello! Have you been swimming?'

'No.'

She wriggled her arm away, laughing at his stern look.

'You can't swim at night can you?'

'No, not really.'

They passed into the lane that led underneath the trees,

and past the view towards the abbey. He pointed up towards the stars beginning to be visible – the Northern Cross. She wasn't all that interested but she liked the intimacy of information.

After their shared fright, he felt close to her. He said, 'Well, will you be sad to leave?'

'Will we come back?'

'Maybe, but just for visits.'

'I don't mind at all.'

Her flat realism amused him suddenly. She reminded him of his father. He laughed at the family resemblance. She laughed too, gratified to have amused him. They walked on silently.

She took his sleeve and said, 'I thought that swan was a ghost.'

He leant towards her confidingly. 'I did too.'

And they walked together towards the admonishing lights of the house, summoning them with luminous reproach for the lateness of the hour.

PART II

Chapter Seven

Being a country state school, this trip to the National Gallery was a rare instance of a cultural outing. For many of those present on this bus, it was their first visit to London and along with the recurrent Bay City Rollers chants, there were many disparaging yells echoing round the back seats, proof of toughness and superiority. Laura sat with Alison, above all this rebellious show, having their own forms unusable on the trip: the Velvet Underground, petty theft, the reading of American poetry and, more recently, soft drug use.

As the bus lurched from gear to gear, and the outskirts of Richmond approached, Laura felt a mixture of superiority and foreboding. She understood that she was expected to be an authority on London, since she had spent so much of her youth there, but her early memories were confined to certain streets only, grey and dutiful walks with Nanny Hart along limited pavement routes. Nowadays it was true she visited the city every holidays, but her explorations were still in the safe and clumsy manner of an astronaut, floating apparently in space while attached to every necessary apparatus still connected to the old world.

Having persuaded her parents that the local town school would provide superior education to her than boarding school (citing as an example the local village school which, following their move, had supplied the first few years of Sussex education), Laura's life for the last three years had been peacefully provincial. Mrs Ruth, who had moved south with them, lived in the village and walked to the Compsons' rented house every day, sleeping there most week nights, Charles and Vivienne only returning from London at weekends.

Mrs Ruth's vagaries prevented the cultivation of local

41

friendship but also prevented knowledge of her deficiencies in this area. She would sometimes meet Laura off the bus from town, and during the walk up the lane would fill her in on the minutiae of school life. She and Laura drifted through the post-school afternoons quite easily, expecting little of each other and being quite content to sit watching television and eating packet puddings together at night. Occasionally Mrs Ruth was able to indulge in regret for the losses of the past, since Laura would not react other than with courtesy, her eye on the television still, spoon imperceptibly nearing the pink glass, feeling no ties to this new temporary home, nor missing the old one. Nanny Hart too had made the initial move with them, but she found that her authority in this county had diminished in some strange way and when she announced her intention to leave after only a few months, it was not as traumatic as might have been imagined.

Martin rarely visited from his school in London, and Laura found it hard to miss him. During the initial months alone, a gulf had sprung up between them and established itself resolutely, widening at a more natural pace at every further gap apart. Their meetings now were routine affairs, enlivened only by casual boasts of wrongdoing on her part – and to her surprise, not so much disbelief as disinterest from Martin.

Her days passed quite peacefully. Occasionally, roused by acts of mild delinquency or the rougher girls' violent enmity towards her grand ways, Laura came alive with the necessity to use her wits, but the rest of the time, she too was in an interim state.

In three months, Laura would move to a smart school in London to do her A-levels, and the very expanse of the city she was moving to hemmed her in when she imagined it, looking out of the coach windows at the lifeless, because unknown, streets. This infinite city shrunk her horizons, in the way the local town had not. Indeed, its small streets had provided endless opportunity, every aspect was explored and used, constructively and the reverse, with the resourceful

Alison. Her house being only a short walk into its outskirts, and Alison's father's dislike of Laura's pedigree notwithstanding, it was restful to end up there for lazy stretches of time, before leaving to catch the bus home. Since she had not had friends of this sort before, Laura looked forward to missing Alison, but she could not prevent the feeling of optimism, the freedom and thrill of loneliness ahead.

They walked through the gallery halls, and then at the entrance to 'Now and Then', their particular exhibition, they were herded together with a lecture on being trusted and the time that they should gather again. The tickets were counted, and they were given permission to enter.

Laura walked ahead, past the old masters and their contemporary counterparts. Most of the paintings bored her and she had no wish to pretend respect just for the sake of it. Then in the last room she paused by one painting: *Sunset Landscape* by Giorgione. She read the description, for some reason interested and then gratified by the dry terms in which the gracefully indolent figures were described. She liked the glimpse of the blue sea in the distance. She read some more and then, having been alerted of their presence, she looked back to the painting to find the visions of the 'monstrous creatures in the lake' that she had missed the first time. There they were – whiskered and charming, apparently unnoticed too by the saints who were fighting dragons, musing and tending to each other with all the listless grace of a dream.

To the side of this painting was its much smaller contemporary pairing and Laura moved to examine that too. It was an infantile painting of flapping black-faced monkeys and unorthodox squatting creatures. It was a disconcerting revelation. It was childishly executed, and perhaps could have been by a child but for its creator being too insistent on the compulsive nature of the grotesque. *Early Birds*. She stood before it; the name Kovel expanded to fill the canvas, pulsing at its edges and entering each creature's ungainly shape.

Alison joined her and sniggered in appreciative manner.

'That's good.'

'Shall we go to the shop?'

'Sure.'

They discussed the evening ahead, and whether Alison should invite over the three 'bus boys' again, recently met and still imperiously referred to as such, the original joke still continued by Alison in spite of her growing intimacy with one of them. But they kept their voices low; they were not immune to the atmosphere of study.

'There's probably not time this evening. Are your parents picking you up from my house?'

'Yes. Then back to London.'

'On your way to visit "the mystic"?'

'Yes.'

Usually Alison liked hearing of Lord Kielder's engaging fancies – his eccentricities described and embellished by Laura were further satisfying aristocratic attributes – and she would have encouraged a return to the subject on the journey home. But today, the prospect of the Compsons' visit to her house restrained her; their self-conscious manner of responding to her little jokes smothered the subject of its usual delicate appeal.

The Walters' front room was small, but that wasn't the most disagreeable factor. Everyone present was conscious of the smell of damp, suggesting not quite poverty but something drabber.

Alison was sniggering in Laura's direction, and Mr Walter stared at the cover of the exhibition catalogue, at the Renaissance swan flapping its inelegant path through the woman's feeble arms. He was able to vent a little of his snobbery.

'So what did you get out of your – cultural *trip*?'

'Oh. It was good!'

Mr Walter certainly couldn't bear that his daughter Alison

was such a dullard, so unattractive compared with the Compson daughter. But listening to her now, he professed to himself, that these recollections and highlights of this National Gallery visit were without Laura's little frills of middle-class charm at least. He had made it his business to see in the Compsons' affectations evidence that they had ideas above their station. He handed the catalogue to Vivienne who examined it with some care.

Referring back to *Early Birds*, Alison's professed choice of favourite, and nodding towards her distantly, Vivienne said, 'The people we're staying with this weekend have an early Kovel too – a portrait of Penelope, the wife. They're friends of his. But I do think these little paintings from that time are his strongest.'

She turned to Mr Walter. 'Do you know his work?'

'Oh yes. I've seen reproductions. He has great appeal to those sections of society that need the novelty of disrespect. Decadence for the middle classes.'

And his wife, Marianne, entering the room with biscuits, and indulging in hostess nerves, looked at him, knowing that this would be a subject that the family would be forced to listen to all night – he really was a most unpleasant man. He was a poet.

Charles cleared his throat, then looking up, saw the refreshments being held before him. He lit up, giggling shyly at having kept her bending down there, tray in hand and having caught his eye, she broke into a coy giggle herself.

He took a cup and a biscuit.

'Oh thank you! Lovely.'

The subject having been raised, Marianne expressed a polite interest in Edward Kielder's books. Mr Walter could not pretend ignorance, as he would have liked, since it would have revealed his provincial limits. The vogue for the last book, *Myths of Albion*, had infuriated him at its zenith five years ago, with its dry Oxford manner, its subtle depiction of the DNA of myth, present in the blades of grass, the mountains, the persistent waves pushing and clawing at the shoreline like a dog with a favourite toy. And the memory of those lines of saints, brought food by ravens in their cavern sanctuaries, walking from their boats with fixed expressions of pious certainty, granting blessings to the lenient wildlife . . .

He looked out of the window, and as if musing, 'Oh, that flabby subject the *past*, the emptier it is, the more it *balloons* out with every fretful little puff into it – !'

Chapter Eight

As they passed the Nottingham turn-off, Laura sat forward. She introduced the subject cautiously, then leant her shoulder against the back of the front seat to look out of the side window, listening to Vivienne's analysis of Christopher Kovel's affair with Edward's sister Jane. Vivienne was short on facts, but enjoying the subject; she turned to answer Laura's occasional casual questions with animation. Charles too felt happy. Since the move down south, these visits to Yorkshire had become something of a yearly tradition; always he felt the reassurance of grandeur within the large ugly construction of the Kielders' house.

Penelope Kielder came hurrying hospitably down the steps to greet them, having heard the crunch of gravel. She took Charles's hands in her own, gave Vivienne a kiss.

'And Laura, how lovely!'

Along the hall she stopped them suddenly with raised hand and with quiet drama, whispered, 'Now I must apologise, the two guests from London, I think, related to each other – he is doing a piece on Edward for some magazine – she is helping him in some way – both (especially her) are a little *tiresome* . . .'

In the sitting-room Edward, having introduced the guests, made a point of sitting and talking to Laura. She found his kind attentions a little burdensome, nevertheless, she liked him and answered his repetitious enquiries courteously enough.

'No, Martin mainly lives with his parents now.'

'Do you miss having a companion, or I suppose you have your school friends.'

'Yes.'

Laura's eyes had remained on Jeanette, the woman from London, since she had a certain interest in those women designated boring.

Penelope came in, saying, 'Shall I show you your rooms?'

Laura liked the corridors, so drab implying space. That they were so dusty, unfinished implied that areas of the house were unseen and unnoticed.

'Will this suit you?'

'Oh, yes – it's the one I always have.'

'Is it, darling? Now, Charles, Vivienne – you're this way . . .'

Laura sat on the brass bed and listened to the faint voices diminishing further along the hall and down the stairs. Lunch would be in half an hour. She got up and shut the door.

She was tired since their early start and feeling slightly sick with her plan. The makeshift packet was at the bottom of her bag, tucked into some folded socks. It had been constructed clumsily, folded in half, quarter, eighth. It had worked, the powder was still there, just visible in the final magazine crease of David Essex's face.

For a moment, something about scraping out and fashioning the drug on the glass top of her familiar bedside table seemed an infringement on the fragile hospitality offered. But Laura had often felt embarrassed that the adult high spirits and chatter in this house seemed to revert to the dull and dutiful when turning towards her. There was no doubt, she was an extra to their pleasure, but now she had her own.

For the first few moments of the effect, she lay back on the white lace cover of the bed and let her mind begin to accelerate. Little bursts of the only other instance of having taken this amphetamine came in – *Metallic KO* from the Stooges in Alison's bedroom and with it now, the apprehension of that recent time. The sinister beat, the lines of white chemically smelling powder laid out by one of the boys and the closed

48

atmosphere – she and Alison had been the only girls – had led Laura to believe that it was some sort of prelude to group sex. Alison had clearly not been fazed, quiet and mocking in her sniggers towards the boy on the floor, but Laura had felt sick with the terror of the song, the drug ritual ahead and its unknown effects. The pounding of her heart had continued after the first line, increasing in spite of the fact that sex had seemed not to be on the cards. Laura knew little of sex, but feeling suddenly reckless, she had known she could have thrown herself in. The powder had mixed with her initial unease and exploded it into potency and she had wanted to celebrate the spirit of decadence of which she felt suddenly equal. But the chemicals were increasingly blowing away from the lower creeping of desire, concentrating all action to the brain.

Up until recently, Laura's only exposure to eroticism, the incident on the beach, had been one of many childhood tales with which Alison had been reliably amused, and she too, by the telling. It had happened so long ago, and, childhood itself being a state deserving of mockery, Laura had raised it through repetition into a mucky myth, more humorous with each telling – there had been three men, all naked, a gun? Oh dear! But that had been some time back. Alison's sexual confidence and ingrained knowledge of the subject was fast eroding the pedestal on which Laura had initially been placed in honour of her exposure to oddity. It seemed now that their favourite was now to be relegated, and like the other infantile amusements, replaced by the adult reality.

Laura's parents had never said, nodding covertly towards her '. . . suddenly she's a grown-up . . .' with the nostalgic pride of a television family. But now, irritation replacing pride, Laura was watching this transformation with Alison. Her subservience was going, she could no longer be relied upon to bow to Laura's cultural delinquency. Instead, she was thoughtful, often smiling to herself as she trudged along, not revealing the joke. And frequently her response to a suggestion was to look away, as if her ambitions were too distant for Laura to see.

Alison had since had sex with one of them, yes, now her 'boyfriend'. But surely the biological actions involved in the sexual act were as matter of fact as coughing? Her dreaminess, the conventional response to its aftermath, must be false and sentimental.

Now as Laura lay there, her arms lying by her sides like an angel, she found her confident exuberance was now leaping ahead of her planning; for a moment she thought the operation blown. And caught up in her mushrooming imaginings, she almost felt inclined to leave matters to fate.

But her mind, in spite of its triumphalism, crept for one shamed instant, back to that scene in Alison's bedroom. Alison was flirting with both boys, and she alone had felt encrusted with the mind's pedantic reasoning. Had she stepped into their midst . . . She had felt damp and unattractive, scared. It was not natural. It was a transformation too much, from mind to body. And anyway, she would be shunned. But still, she had felt the stirrings of arousal, the wish to be natural. Instead she had turned to the books piled up on the table, picked up one and leaning, stared out of the window at the dusk birds whirring with businesslike intensity.

A consolation had come to her. She had foreseen that despite her lack of progress in normal life, lying ahead would be a remarkable destination, some forbidding landscape, in which she with her exposure to extremes would feel at home, to be greeted and welcomed by its other curious inhabitants.

Having heard noises of imminent departure, she had turned away from the window, watched the last lines being laid out, but at once she had felt impatient, the fury of all prophets – the time would come, but when? To hasten this end was the desired option. And to make sure that should it rise up into sight, she should have every advantage available to make haste to its end. And in the confusion of goodbyes and plans being made by the door, Laura had scraped half of her line into the magazine poster, quite able to look up with a casual goodbye too, as she folded it into her pocket for just such future provision as now had come.

On her own, on a mission, even the dark corners of these private corridors seemed potent. Every encroached room was empty – but this one? And there, above the bookcase was the painting that she had seen on these past occasions – the exposed breast then just another still life.

The address book was on the desk and on top of it was the familiar little tin toy, the checked golfer, intent on his impending swing. Before putting it to one side, she pulled back the spring, and his club flew up in professional readiness, but in the interests of discretion, she allowed it to return without the satisfaction of a noisy putt.

Running her thumb down to K, she opened the book fully at that section. She wanted none of the hastiness that would indicate guilt should she be caught. But there, on the second frayed page of K, was his name. The information was crossed out, a newer address fitted in underneath, only the word 'Christopher' diagonally beside it. She found it somewhat disgusting, the ease of this casual intimacy – it thrilled her! She allowed herself the one time-wasting daydream – that one day she too would have the authority to write the information with the same casual breeziness: 17 King Street, Highgate Hill, Highgate.

She glanced back up at the painting. She felt superstitiously disinclined to spend long on examination, she knew too well the price exacted for indulgence over duty, but her heart beat faster at the recognition of similar attributes in this one to *Early Birds* – surely there was no mistaking his peculiar emphases?

'Hello!'

Laura, with imbecilic grace, picked up and placed the tin golfer back on the address book to confuse her observer. She felt that Edward was equally startled at finding her in that room. She kept her eyes upward, as if in studious examination.

'I was looking at that painting.'

He looked up and stared in silence too.

She said, 'It's very good, isn't it?'

'It certainly took a lot of work to do.'

'You know the artist?'

'He's a friend of my sister Jane.'

'Is that her?'

'No – that's Penelope with our newly born Tom! Shall we go and get our lunch?'

Edward was bored by the chatter of his guest, doing his utmost to adapt to aristocratic whimsy. Having spent the day before at a neighbouring estate, in order to interview its owner too, he was full of eccentric tales, badly told. Edward cleared his throat and turned to the silent group following behind in crocodile fashion.

'I was saying that you should be interviewed too, Charles, for this magazine. I'm sure you have a few tales of ancestral oddity.'

Charles pursed up his face in a childish effort of memory.

'A few . . .'

Equally childish in his inelegance, the man shifted ingratiatingly.

'Unfortunately, my terrible editors only want titled subjects – oh the perils of attempting a literary living!'

The path widened somewhat and as the others stood in a group, listening to a tale, Laura and Edward's brother Archie walked on together side by side. He stumped along, deep in silence. The lake glistened in the distance and beyond it the outline of the uncompromising northern hills seemed from the time before hand of man intervened – grander and more indicative of God than the cosier cluttered south.

'Do you believe that King Arthur visited here?'

'It wasn't King Arthur, but no I don't. I think that most of my brother's theories are absolute rubbish.'

'Oh.'

'Absolute rubbish to tack on meaning where there is none. Things just are what they are.'

'So are you a modern art lover?'

'Really I don't have time for art at all. Except for the very old works that have *stood the test of time*.'

'So what do you have time for?'

Penelope's voice came from the back of the group –

'Here we are, Charles – *this is where we stop!*'

Charles stopped automatically, finishing, 'Sometimes I miss it, yes – but I have my other life now.'

He and Jeanette stood in the clearing, waited the few minutes for the rest of the group to catch up. Seeing that they were not taking advantage of the chairs, hidden in the thick ferns, Penelope pushed herself forward to the front of the group, so as to pull back the leaves and reveal their convenient presence.

'Please – let's all sit here for a minute!'

'Isn't this lovely!'

The magazine writer's supercilious voice rang out over the clearing, managing to spoil its delicate charm by pointing it out in such a fashion.

Laura lay on the ground. All around nature teemed and overran. The flies hung in the air or flitted back to the water. Perhaps the grown-ups were looking at her, perhaps not.

'Well, it's funny you should ask – poor old boy. Such a sad ending, really something more should have been done for him. By our royals perhaps.'

'Did you ever come across him in your research?'

'Who's that?'

'King Freddie of Africa.'

'No, I'm not sure I did.'

His laugh cautiously felt its way forward.

'But you write articles on royalty, don't you?'

'Oh, Archie – your voice gave me a start, not often heard but when it is . . .!'

'Not really featuring non-*European* royals I'm afraid . . .'

'He's as royal as anyone else, considering the whole institution is man-made in the first place.'

'His grandfather, on an official visit to England, indicated that the delightful crocodiles, fed by hand in the private zoo by he and his entourage, would be acceptable as a gift from their owner, Queen Victoria. I rather like that. You see, I sometimes think it's their African over-enthusiasm, such a lovely trait – that leads people not to think of them as truly royal. And Laura – you remember Freddie I'm sure – you would love his book *Desecration of My Kingdom* – have you read the *Odyssey*?'

'No.'

'I'm going to make a note – I'll give it to you before you go. In both, similar beliefs in magic, savagery, honour and ritual – and the return to a beloved homeland.'

'But not for poor old Freddie.'

After a while, Laura fell asleep, and in her dream they argued exhaustedly, stepping over her to the lake and stepping over her back again.

'So you could say he died of love . . . But, after all, what is love?'

'Convenience.'

'Oh, Archie – such romance!'

'Oh all the bits and pieces fit together *well enough* – and then it works all right.'

Before she could answer, Laura was woken by the voice of Penelope saying that perhaps they'd better return to the house, since tea would soon be laid on.

Charles woke in the threadbare armchair, the sensation of his dream still unsettling. Outside the window, the tops of green leaves were losing their brilliance with the light. He smoothed its shiny chintz arms in the dainty way he sometimes had. He looked around the blue and yellow walls.

'So, tea ready?'

'I suppose.'

Vivienne was moving from one end of the room to the other, fussing with her clothes.

He said, 'God, what a strange dream.'

'You always say that, and they're always about gardening or the dog.'

'No . . .'

But he found that,before forming the words, he held back, embarrassed.

'Actually, I now can't remember really.'

'Good, there's nothing so dreary as dreams. Unless –'

Vivienne lowered her voice amusingly – '(You count the wallpaper in this room.)'

'Mm.'

He wished that she would not feel obliged to carry her artificial manner into their private life. He found it simpler to agree, because he loved the room – full of brash colours and of course, tasteless. The whole large house was consistently free of the wearisome vacillations of style. He yawned and asked.

'So, nice visit?'

'About the same as ever.'

'Ah well, shall we go down now?'

'No, not even time for muffins I'm afraid!'

Jeanette followed the writer in his swift progress round the table, giving no one a chance to snub them by not rising, shaking hands and professing pleasure.

'I hope we meet in London!'

Jeanette looked from Charles to Vivienne. Charles pushed back his chair, half stood to give her a parting kiss.

'Please let's do that! We'll give you a call.'

The couple left the room with Edward, and once their voices were far enough away the remaining company turned on Charles with bemused laughter.

'There's no need to be *that* polite!'

'Oh, Vivienne – they were dreadful – I'm sorry to subject you to them, but, Charles, you were marvellous, thank you.'

When Edward returned, the talk was still hilariously critical. He looked bemused.

'They aren't that bad, well, he isn't . . .'

'They *are* that bad, you just like him because he listened to your stories for hours on end.'

'Talked my ear off for hours on end you mean!'

Penelope stood back mockingly aghast.

'Well – you see! And Charles – what on earth did you find to say to her? – Laura, I know, what must you think – can you have had any fun out of this visit at all?'

Laura was laughing, flattered by the assumption that she too would have found this couple boring.

'Do you want to come with us – I am going to borrow your father, ask his advice on a gardening matter.'

'No. It's OK. Could I have another explore round?'

'My dear girl – help yourself! Now, Charles, I know you have green fingers . . .'

She took his arm and led him out of the room, along the corridor and out into the walled garden, talking of old times, Edward's new book, their son Tom just finishing at Eton. The garden had the last square of the setting sun in one corner. Charles suggested cutting back the jasmine or moving it to a sunnier wall.

'Moving it! Well, you're probably right.'

They talked a little of old friends – and her sister-in-law Jane and her husband, Paul Sikorski, and of his mysterious financial dealings outside his rather successful dining club off Albemarle Street.

'Has Paul approached you for financial involvement at any time?'

'Other than membership of "The Club" – nothing – I'm not in his league I'm afraid.'

'I think perhaps that's not altogether a bad thing . . .'

They discussed Jane who was still, yes (as far as she knew), conducting her illicit romance with Christopher Kovel.

'I don't know what Paul makes of it – if he even knows . . . I never see him, oh sometimes Jane – she brought Christopher here once – and you think him good, Charles, do you?'

'Oh yes. Rather like him too.'

'Yes, well he's certainly got something.'

She knew that she and Edward were considered amusing, he for his theories and she for her placidity. The myth of her one time wildness, evinced by the portrait in the library, was a source of quiet pleasure, but quite erroneous. She had sat for this painting with her newly born son Tom. She had agreed with no fuss to be painted breast-feeding, since the ladies of her circle, including the younger Jane, had been so adamant. When the finished work was presented, she lived up to all expectations by scrutinising it quietly, observing finally, 'Beautiful colours.'

And had turned to see the artist exchanging amused looks with the other two women present, her friends.

Chapter Nine

Christopher Kovel had spread a strong and invulnerable net of privacy, but some communications slipped through. He found letters of praise tiresome, but there were far fewer of those. His paintings were seen by most as being a revelation of the brutality of matter, thoroughly dissected and spread out as if on a forensic table. To those of a sensitive nature, this slap across the face of polite English conviction might have been uplifting, but to those more confident about the world, his works were an affront, his skilled technique only rendered the subject matter and approach all the more loathsome. These last sorts of critics were loud in their condemnation; the world moving increasingly towards admiration of the lowest view of life and they felt obliged to argue this point with angry examples of optimism.

His West End gallery tried their best to marry discretion and integrity. Though legally they could not obey his request to throw letters addressed to him away, nor did they have the time to deal with them themselves, they occasionally mislaid the more obviously insane ones.

Today he received two letters, the first via the gallery he threw away unopened since he could tell by the handwriting what sort of drivelling litany of disapproval it would be likely to contain. The second, sent directly to his address, he opened since the unknown handwriting was youthful. It was a letter of praise, written with an attempt at sophistication. 'I got your address out of the Kielders' address book, I hope you don't mind, you can always ignore this letter.'

But he had no intention of ignoring it. He was annoyed but he considered that the fingers that had crept towards this unforgivable breach of privacy, might in the future, have the

inclination to spread themselves in more satisfactory delinquency –

'This is giving me a most hideous rash . . .'

Scratching at the arms of his grey wool dressing-gown,
Jane came in, stared at the pheasant lying beside the sink. He
watched her with sudden animation pluck a small bunch of
feathers out of the breast. She was a particularly subtle and
discriminating cook, an art Christopher appreciated. More
usually, her indolence placed her on a high plain of frivolity,
way above the cares of domesticity. She had never shown any
inclination to try to prevent his other romances, but he
slipped the letter into his pocket with a blank look that she
ignored. She found the energy having to be expended on her
own married life tiresome enough, even the little that her
husband, Paul, demanded.

'It hasn't been hung for long enough. Who provided it?'

His answer was almost inaudible since he hated providing
even the most innocuous domestic information.

'Joan Anthony.'

'That repulsive old toad – Oh *well* . . . '

She scratched both arms one after the other with exaggerated wrath.

'Why you like this ghastly dressing-gown I fail to understand.'

She pulled the sleeve down enough so that he could see the
red rash.

'Invisible . . .'

She laughed her coarse infectious laugh and he pushed the
dressing-gown further off her shoulders, placed his hands
reflectively on her breasts. She rested her forehead on his.
Her laugh to Christopher, like her unorthodox cooking
skills, suggested a world of aristocratic abandon, the bits and
pieces of which still added up to some considerable sum of
glamour.

'Do you want to go on working?'

'I'd like to if we may.'

59

Pulling the gown back on, she went ahead and he followed, pausing on route to deposit the letter under a pile of papers in his study. He would reply to it at a later date.

In the studio Jane now sat reading on the day bed, wearing the flowered shirt. She watched as he picked up the discarded dressing-gown from the floor and put it on the patched green leather chair, another testament to his esoteric taste. Not only celebrated for drawing ugliness from the commonplace, he was also wilfully drawn to the already unattractive, his choices, it was understood, bestowing a certain charm even on these unlikely artefacts.

Chapter Ten

Holding the letter in her lap, Laura stared at the wallpaper of her small rented room. She had at once guessed the sender from the handwriting on the envelope. Her name was quite as strangely spelt out as she could have hoped – as if a precocious monkey were making a painful effort for the few seconds his concentration allowed. Not for this one the melodious flourishes that are bound to lead to disappointment if calligraphy is any indication of character, nor the normal manner of conveyance, it had been pushed through the front door.

She waited for a further moment, fearful of its contents. But inside, it was brief and definite – he would like to see her. She felt sick reading the modest reproof 'I don't like being hunted down.' But he ended it by agreeing with her suggestion that they meet. He would be at the bar at Wheelers at seven o'clock on Wednesday, the following evening.

Laura blushed and put the letter down. She had had some small triumphs in her life. But none like this, the first intimation of the taste of actual success. Her heart pounding, she was conscious of the dread of the follow-up that might go wrong and ruin the thrill of this future. She respected secrecy and had no wish to tell anyone of this awkward manifestation of good fortune; anyway, there were few that she could tell.

She had sent the letter only a month ago, she had hoped that by waiting London would have instilled in her some necessarily unusual qualities that would be recognised by such as he. And then, as month after month had gone by, the loneliness of unpopularity had flattened her confidence altogether.

At first, Laura's protestations of this unpopularity, amusingly described, had filled her parents with a sort of pride. Having for the past ten years indulged her wish to go to local

61

schools, they had chosen the school in London for every good reason, but were quite prepared to agree that its occupants were insufferable. Indeed, they looked forward to further stories of her alienation within its middle-class enclaves. But as the months had gone on, the manifestation of this alienation, her constant availability, had begun to drive Vivienne into making irritable and rather too frequent enquiries into her spasmodic social life.

But still she could make no inroads into the strange world of her school contemporaries. Many of them knew each other already, and anyway groups had soon been formed, within which the conventions were slipped into easily. Their attempts at eccentricity frightened her. They were polite enough when they spoke to her, rudeness she would have understood. But something about their shrivelling looks of disinterest and occasionally disgust at her manifestations of energy, enthusiasm and wrongly placed cynicism was familiar.

The only other girl to be taking S-level English was sternly indifferent to these hierarchies and for that reason Laura quite liked her. One afternoon, walking together, they had chatted quite amicably about Becky Sharp having married the wrong Crawley, but at Laura's suggestion of a drink at the pub they were passing, she had returned to blank disapproval, and wandered on. But that night back in her room, the vodka Laura had drunk had risen and unsteadily toppled the habitual mortification. She had got up from her bed, written the letter and without reading it again (how often had that led to dismay and scrunched up pieces of paper!) had sealed it and gone downstairs to the local post-box. In a fit of triumphalism, she had followed this with a visit to the local pub for another round, but this drink had left her slightly sick and unable to sleep.

For weeks there had been no response, nothing had happened and her mortification having returned, there was a small sluggish hope that nothing would. But even during those empty times, she had yet been conscious of the one leap into faith that remained like a carved saint placed randomly within an otherwise secular construction, its blank eyes staring incomprehensibly into space, giving neither guidance nor knowledge. It remained there still, a faith now fulfilled.

It was getting too late and finally Laura emerged from her room. Mrs Golde Madison left off from her kitchen tasks and came towards her admiringly. Folding the tea towel on the sideboard, she turned her around by her shoulders then held her in place for a proper look. It was an intimacy that would have been inconceivable when Laura first took up paying residence with her; pity had broken through her Nordic reserve. She nodded sagely.

'Well, I hope you have a special evening dressed like that!'

Laura had settled on a dress that billowed as she walked. It was black and expensive, borrowed from her mother some time back. She put faith in the label and that the original choice of purchase had been her mother's. But its unsuitability was confirmed twenty-five minutes later by the swish of the door, rushed and opened by a smirking waiter, catching his colleagues' eyes and making much of this party-dressed young lady.

She asked if – she didn't like to say his name since the few customers there at that early hour were looking at her. And then towards the back she saw a small grey figure hovering, neither standing, nor hardly looking her way. She raised her eyebrows in a small question, imperceptibly returned, and the headwaiter swooped to collect her from his position behind the bar.

They didn't stay long at Wheelers; Christopher took Laura to the familiar French pub, two streets further on. It was crowded and he left her to buy champagne and water for himself. It was packed with the sort of drinkers that prided themselves on world-weariness; the old men raised their eyebrows, their mouths remained turned down towards their drinks – a young girl in a pretty dress. One of the drinkers in the far corner was a friend of Christopher's, but he had no wish to join them. Instead he remained, looking at the girl from his hidden vantage point; he felt irritated by the inevitability of habit. Then she sat and disappeared from his view.

His companion who had waved to them from this convivial-looking corner now chattered and pushed his way through, and Laura recognised him from his time as an actor on a children's television programme. Her shyness made him pay attention to her, creating a false impression of the evening ahead.

'Christopher and I have been coming here for – what, twenty years? This place has blossomed by nature of its scruffy appeal to artistic types, meaning drunkards (and paupers of a rather charming aspect!)'

He leered familiarly, evidently referring to himself.

'Shall we . . . ?'

They left and walked towards his shabby grey van in silence. He got in. It was cold and she felt sick. She climbed through the open passenger door and the van set off immediately – almost as if sharing her shy wish for privacy. But no, another glance at his furious face, ignoring her pleasantries with stimulating rudeness, gazing with indifference into the driving mirror at the ineffectual bicycle bell trills following their progress, his social inhibitions could not be attributed to shyness.

He was tired. Christopher's reserves of energy were almost limitless, but the night before he had given up even the small amount of sleep necessary in order to work on a painting of Jane. The plan had been that she stay and sit for him that night, but her husband, Paul, had returned a day early and had asked that she join him for a business dinner at his club. Christopher had thought that her absence would mean finishing some aspects of the background. But suddenly the painting had started to go wrong, and without her presence it was impossible to see if it could be salvaged. His dislike of her husband was a familiar theme, and as Christopher scraped the work furiously further into mediocre oblivion, the cheap snobbery that had led to Paul's insistence on Jane's presence at this dinner enraged him again.

'You know them, don't you?'

He had heard fragments of Laura's background chat – it had been about her family.

'Yes. I like Charles.'

'But not so keen on mum . . . ?'

'I don't really know her.'

He turned down a small street with such urgency that he seemed unable to answer her next question about where they were going.

'I thought we would go back . . .'

His flat was on the top floor. On the way up the stairs, he placed a hand on Laura's neck, almost pushing. Outside his door, he slid past her to deal with the three locks, placing his hand back on her neck as he did so, necessitating that the operation was lengthened even further.

He allowed her then through the open door, and sidled away from her reaction. It was very neat and the European furniture was dark and unappealingly delicate. There was a functional smell of paint, presumably coming from one of the closed doors on the next half floor up.

'Do you want . . . ?'

She liked the way the champagne was slightly flat, and courageously persisted in her lightheartedness.

'I like that!'

She pointed towards one corner of the hall, at the upside-down felt elephant, rather formal except for a little scarlet hat.

He hunched up his shoulders in a little laugh.

'It was a present – I'm painting one, you see.'

He wound his arms around her not with affection but with purpose. She thought of the fumbling she had experienced previously – but for all her relief at his deft expertise, she couldn't prevent the memory of a dutiful man she had witnessed as a child, flat on his stomach, hoisting with urgent impatience, a large dog out of a pond.

The cars hooted at them gratifyingly as they ran through the slow-moving traffic of Trafalgar Square. Martin skipped up the steps delightedly. Although he found Laura's protestations of school unpopularity unappealing, feeling himself not to be doing so well in that area himself, he still found it hard to resist her unorthodox approach to shocking subjects.

'Really? He did that?'

He was in paroxysms of laughter, and wasn't sure he wanted to see the marvellous picture that had inspired the hunt for its creator; he wasn't inclined to swap such hilarity for reverence.

But the exhibition she wanted of 'Now and Then' had long finished. Laura was most disappointed, considered it a bad omen. She had very much wanted to have some acclaim for her conquest along with this amusement. But they went back to the shop by the main entrance. There she skimmed through a few contemporary art books on the middle table, and finally found a recent photograph. Martin peered closely over her shoulder and then withdrew his head.

'A bit older than I'd thought.'

She had one more look at the sour grey-faced man, her good mood gone because it was true.

She agreed to walk round some of the rooms anyway, since they were there. And wandering around the halls, she felt charmed and comforted again in small doses by the little people in the paintings who were up to all sorts of foolish stuff or lying around after sex looking a bit dim. She supposed them to have just had sex. But painters in those days certainly approached nudity in a far from erotic manner. Certainly there was none of the crude violence and excitable disgust present that she recognised as being a sexual approach; not filthy at all, these figures were produced cautiously and with respect.

66

Then at last she found herself again in front of *Sunset Landscape* that, as she had feared, had lost some of its extreme ability to shock her. But she really was still most charmed in a way that she couldn't quite understand by the monsters almost submerged there in the middle of the delicate countryside. She felt a certain gratitude towards the whims of its creator, and the creation of all subjects there. And she just liked looking around; the descent of the grace of God, the wolf of Gubbio so obediently penitent.

Chapter Eleven

At first their romance was sporadic; they met once or twice a month. Laura could hear the telephone ringing from her small bedroom down the hall. But if, lying on her green counterpane, she heard her landlady Mrs Golde Madison's manner change from brisk to furiously engrossed, expectation would start her heart racing.

Soon after, there would be the expected knock at the door.

'It's that man again, who *still* refuses to give his name.'

One night Laura told Christopher of Mrs Golde Madison's distress and scored an unexpected success. He was amused by her name and Laura's tales of her frustration with his secrecy.

She embellished some more, adding the truthful, 'She didn't used to like me, but this has made her.'

This flimsy bond was strengthened that New Year's Eve – Laura having told him the family was away, complied uneasily with his whim to explore the place. She felt guilty showing him round their finicky flat, but having completed the brutal and somewhat laboured sexual act on the tiny bed next to the kitchen, she felt that their laughter at this delinquency was rather a special secret.

But back at his flat, the intimacy left as if it had never existed. In the kitchen, Laura watched his nervous back, at the sink, trimming the brussel sprouts that had been lying on the kitchen table, fresh from a friend's garden. But this expensive champagne, in her own half-bottle, was an acknowledgement of her individual desires. She felt it was too intimate to say how good it was, to draw attention to it at all. Always on shaky ground, this signalled she hoped, the suggestion of a move towards an official relationship.

Having dealt with the sprouts, and now waiting for them to boil, Christopher sat down at the table, looking at the chair next to his, reading a newspaper that was lying there. With a quick glance at her, he put on his old woman's spectacles. This emboldened Laura to tell him about the painting that she had chosen to write on for this month's art history essay – Giorgione's *Sunset Landscape*. She had assumed that having been paired with his painting for the one time and pre-eminent National Gallery exhibition, it was a safe bet. She thought she was getting nowhere since his face, though no longer peering at the newspaper, was screwed up in discomfort at the direction of the table, perhaps discomforted at being taken from his paper she thought. But he took off his glasses, looked at her distantly.

'That painting is third rate –'

Christopher, usually the least amenable of acquaintances, had taken some considerable pains to secure the loan of his early painting from its Japanese owner as had been requested for that particular show. It was a considerable tribute to the administrator's charm that Christopher had not, on hearing of his planned juxtaposition, refrained from these efforts. The arguments as to the subtlety of the allegory made no inroads into changing his opinion as to Giorgione's abilities, rather the reverse, since it was the artist's soppy symbolism that Christopher held most contemptible.

This last he explained now. He was not critical of Laura for having chosen the painting, but he was repelled that it had appeared as a subject to be discussed in his kitchen. Laura, though chastened, could see that the argument had taken on a life of its own, and so she could listen without too much shame, knowing that the disappointment could wait till later.

'. . . as if popularity were in any sense, an indication of merit.'

'Yes, I see.'

He rose from his chair, back towards the oven, saying in a

soft courteous murmur, 'Do you mind if tonight you don't spend the night here? I have to work first thing in the morning.'

'Not at all.'

He returned, bent his head down, his glasses firmly on, to continue with his newspaper article, only springing up to take the brussel sprouts off the boil. He sprinkled them onto a white plate with some oil and salt and placed this delicately down in front of her to have with her wine and pheasant. As she took some and began to eat, he looked anxiously at his watch and she realised her time was nearly up. She finished and stood but before she could leave to dress, he blocked her path. It seemed that he had something he wished to say.

'I'd like to paint you if I may?'

'Certainly.'

And social accomplishment was there too! In the very casual manner of her assent, she knew she had successfully curtailed all but a very fraction of her happiness.

Chapter Twelve

The dog had been allowed to accompany them into the dining car, permission had been granted by a drunkenly sluttish young guard who had bent to pet him with what should have been a warning signal of extravagant incoherence.

As they waited for their food, Charles had watched his antics with sly pleasure, glancing from time to time towards the other diners. But then the dog ventured too far into the aisle and the obsequious old waiter righted himself and cursed. He ordered it removed from the dining car in tones of Scottish vituperation, the pitch of which had descended into spiteful self-pity, quite commensurate with the flavour of their wretched outing.

A month ago, in the first excitement of grief, Charles had agreed that a little service of remembrance for his father, to be held in the private chapel in the grounds of the abbey, would be appropriate. But now he regretted that gesture. He had no wish to return whatever the circumstance and these circumstances were peculiarly false and sentimental.

Charles's relationship with his father had deteriorated over the years into something like indifference. Only the presence of Vivienne would produce animation in either of them. Alone together in a room, they would sit silent, Charles suffuse with inadequate irritation and Hilary in his own dreams of money-making.

His wife's death had left him an unanticipated amount of capital, most of which Hilary had spent in a surprisingly short time on schemes that he did not recognise as being enjoyable. His disapproval of frippery had allowed him the freedom to spend it in great blocks.

Now he was dead, and what little money would remain

after taxes and debts had been cleared had been left to Laura. The Scottish property belonged to the bank and the London flat had been left to Charles. The idea was put forward by Vivienne that Laura should buy the London flat from Charles with this money left to her. She would soon be eighteen and, after all, she would need a place of her own. This idea had strengthened during the informal lawyer's meeting at the time of the Scottish funeral. The lawyer, with gloom, had pushed his large hands over his face, had confessed that this might not be the most efficient route – there were inheritance taxes to be dealt with (he looked down shamefaced) and debts. Charles had attended the local village school until the age of eight and so had understood his reticence to be an obscure tribute to the presence of death. But as to this suggestion – Charles had seen the very real benefits of the arrangement. It was a perfectly good flat, but not especially marketable – being indifferently laid out and somewhat dilapidated from lack of use. With a look towards Laura, he had suggested that until it became impossible, that they should proceed along this route? Laura had agreed; she had seemed polite but indifferent. In fact, she had felt relief that her opinion was scarcely sought, she wanted the debate to draw to a close and she quite liked decisions being made for her. And when these decisions were not entirely to her benefit, she could relax in the freedom of constraint.

But now, on the train, listening to this *fait accompli* and Vivienne's efforts to cajole her into enthusiasm, some little invasion was taking place – some little fucking instinct gamely pulsing its way into life against the efforts to suppress it. It was enough that it was done – the idea that she should be thrilled at the prospect of decorative flourish! Vivienne, seeing that her efforts to enthuse were going unrewarded, moved to a more immediately gratifying task – notification of the arduous work ahead, cleaning and so on. And this had some effect, since Laura turned to stare out of the train window.

She was filled with supernatural terrors quite unsuited to her dull memories of the place. All she could think of were the spidery strands that would grow and reveal themselves when the cleaning started. She could hardly blame them, but the old gave up their interest in cleanliness; they grew immune to dirt, knowing after all, that it would soon be their entire surrounds.

The chapel was on the edge of the park and few landmarks needed to be passed to reach it. Inside it was filled with those members of staff who still remained, a few local friends and two representatives of the present administrative team, who hung their heads in dignified solemnity, knowing the responsibility of usurped ownership. Even the arrival of Lord and Lady Kielder did not stir them into any shared smile.

Laura had known Edward for much of her life as a droll but distant adult, but increasingly, since moving to her new school, Laura liked to hear further details of his strange beliefs, laughing in anticipation when the subject was broached by Charles who liked to see her amused. She had heard the name of his son Tom being mentioned by the more popular girls at school, but she was unable to gain a foothold by pretending that she knew him too. The best that she could come up with was that she could think of herself as a friend of his family at least. Once, on hearing two girls talk of staying with him, she had interrupted politely, corrected one of them when they had used Tom's surname 'Kilnsea' for his parents. She hadn't been arrogant – but her eagerness had been obvious and the two girls had nodded, turned away to talk animatedly again of more intense matters.

Now Laura felt shy seeing Edward in person, looking far from ludicrous, but smiling with appropriate melancholy in the pew opposite. She wondered if he knew about the illicit means to her romance, previously dismissed in her mind as an unimportant necessity.

After the service they stood outside the chapel, and she

hung back alone, listening to the greetings and expressions of regret from those members of the staff who still lived on the estate. The famous landmark wasn't visible from this point, but still she could see that the grounds were lovely.

Edward, seeing her alone, came up.

'So sad, so sad . . .'

He looked around at the trees, smiling.

She said shyly, gesturing towards the direction of the abbey, 'I remember when you came over for lunch with King Freddie and showed us the site of the saint's burial place . . .'

'Oh, do you? Do you?'

But before she could venture further into this treasured and apparently safe anecdote, Charles brought Mr Harding up for a reunion and the moment was lost. As Laura listened to his memories of the old days, reminiscing herself about the dog's first entrance into the library, Edward took Charles aside, said that he'd heard that he was starting a new venture.

'Yes – and it sounds rather good . . .'

But before he could continue on this confidential note, Edward held up his hands with a comical, 'No use explaining business schemes to me (although of course, I'm not entirely without business know-how . . .)'

He raised his face from thought, added amiably, 'But be careful with my brother-in-law now, Charles. I feel Paul's mind won't be on this tentative venture as much as yours – he's a successful man!'

Charles nodded. At the intimation of warning in the subject being broached, Charles had thought he was being warned off – but it was too unfortunate a subject and one that he was shortly going to have to bring up with Laura herself.

At first, Charles and Vivienne had disregarded all evidence pointing towards Laura's affair, but the rumours kept coming, since there were few of their acquaintances who could resist the rare gratification of disapproval. Eventually it had been Martin's mother, Anne, who had felt obliged to voice her concerns directly. Having deliberated, she had felt herself to be family enough that it *was* her business. Her cautious but deliberate words were met with assumed cognition and nonchalance, but after that Charles and Vivienne had been forced to acknowledge that the affair was real. They had talked about it, and the most promising conclusion that they had come to was that Laura was testing the water, dipping her toe into the pool of sexual delinquency.

Both knew Christopher slightly, had followed his latest romances and had defended him on occasion in the face of philistine disapproval. Charles had always taken shy pleasure in being able to greet him but he now felt that all his pleasure was being thrown back in his face.

Charles had suggested they go for a walk and the dog ran along, too old now to be imaginative. As they wandered along the path, he made a couple of remarks concerning her new flat, and Laura answered with a polite show of enthusiasm.

Charles had the admirable ability to ignore unpleasant facts or feelings if that were at all possible, thus banishing them. Walking along these paths that he once owned gave him no trouble at all although his face was set. He allowed his fingers to brush against the hanging wisps of leaf. He was abashed at the prospect of their talk; sex was not a subject he found easy, unless it was placed within a mildly humorous context.

He broached the subject of her attachment in a most matter-of-fact way; he presented it as a mild statement of fact and she agreed that it was so.

They were in the shade of the wood, and ahead beckoned the open lawns leading to the abbey and the sea. It was not seemly to talk of such things outside; nature was not at all suitable. But since the cover of shade was about to be lost he asked, 'Well, if he's going to paint you, do you think it could be with some clothes on?'

His embarrassment and the rare nature of the request touched Laura; he so rarely asked for any modification of behaviour. She agreed with the minimum of explanation. But the thought that she was already being discussed in those terms – as one of Christopher's future fallen – to be sprawled in ungainly discomfort for the gleaming eyes of art lovers! No, it was too intoxicating an addition to her dreams. And as they continued towards the abbey, every glittering grey stone revealed itself, presenting its treasures up to her with the creaking dignity of a once-revered hero. And she responded with the correct honour – bowing her head to glimpse from left to right – she came from this – from this! She had been right, it was predestined that such spectacular origins would have set her up for an unusual future.

Laura spent the evening of her return with some girls from school and some male friends of theirs. They never had disliked her – they were quite prepared to accept her since in most ways she fitted the bill of their conventional standards of good looks and connections, but she could see that they found her surges of enthusiasm trying. In this instance they all were sympathetic to her loss, and she built up on that with a description of the service; neither grief-stricken or dismissive, she managed to project the right amount of stoicism. But success of this accidental dignity went to her head – and she lost her audience again with her flippant account of the flat soon to be hers. The pride in her grandparent's absence of taste was missed, she appeared spoilt.

She tried to blend in again, she had enjoyed that fleeting moment of alignment, but the boys eyed her with some sort of mistrust as she joined in with their erotic humour of asides and vulgar allusion. She could see by their irritable avoidance techniques that they found her unattractive, but even allowing for the most rigorous self-analysis, she still couldn't quite see why.

She thought of her last Sussex school where her differences had seemed occasionally stimulating. And of those small group of boys, who had gathered around she and Alison in the bus station that afternoon, forming bonds based on appreciation for the Beatles' *White Album*. Now she thought of them and no longer felt she had since moved above a juvenile crowd. She missed the sulphate too that had become a regular feature of their Saturdays in the last two months of that school, even if it had always left her dried out and depressed the next day. Cocaine she had recently tried at a party, and it seemed a more subtle drug, but unlike those old country days she didn't hang out with a gang in which it was prevalent – or any gang at all. Many nights, alone in her little room, she got drunk. She had learned that a bottle of red wine just pushed her into a different form of melancholy, a more acceptable one. In company she felt agitated after a few glasses. There was always a moment when she thought she had discovered confidence but it grew out of proportion by the third or fourth glass and she couldn't quite escape the effect on the others present.

'Do you like *Metallic KO* by the Stooges?'

'Don't know it.'

'At the end of "Louie Louie", the last song, he gets knocked unconscious by a bottle.'

'Oh.'

She suggested a second bottle of wine from the off-licence and insisted on going herself, noticing as she did so, the looks exchanged at the suggestion. At the local off-licence, she flirted with the Indian man serving; he suggested 'A party afoot?' But she held up the quarter bottle of whisky jauntily – 'No, this is for *me*!' He laughed in sympathy.

Outside, she drank it down in one. Bloated and drunk and she stank. That was about it. Walking was all right at night and so she swaggered along Gloucester Road. Now she was drunk, she could face her passing reflection in the shop windows and admit it, she was puffed out with a coating of sweat and alcohol. And about to cross the road, she had to wait for a minute as a van drove at some erratic speed towards her. It slowed as it drew alongside and the familiar driver turned to look at her with venomous intensity, before continuing on with his urgent and noisy journey down the narrow Kensington Road. She had looked back impassively and she felt proud of this. Her subsequent replay lingered on his intensity and cut around his great age and his female companion. It was a look of recognition after all, that he had thrown her; and it was recognition that she was after. Recognition of her unusual attributes, one of which was patience, another – indifference.

Always in the middle of the sitting, Christopher would come over very matter-of-factly, like making an irritable cup of tea, and fuck her. She would often be asleep since the pose was one in which she lay on the sofa with her eyes closed, covered by a blue wool jacket. In her sleep, she would hear his boots approaching, her body informing her mind of what was about to take place, tensing slightly at the familiar clank of the steps. She would feel the jacket being removed with no sense of surprise and would enter into the whole procedure without having to think much about it. Today she had been in the middle of a dream, which though unpleasant in some undefined way, she had wished to stay with. His insistent fingers were unwelcome, dragging her from a discussion on the creatively lazy dark matter – like a child with a conscientiously critical parent examining a recent effort dropped for easier pastimes. Her father had looked up, held up a finger.

'. . . but where's the part that holds it up?'

'It's there, but invisible.'

She woke full of the foreboding that had been specific enough that she would have preferred to remain there. She pushed his hands away and sat up, but he continued with scarcely a pause, just enough that she should be relatively still again.

After it he suggested they take a break.

'I might have a bath?'

He had no wish to refuse, but his agitation could scarcely be contained, when after twenty minutes, he went in and found her still lying unmoving in the water staring at the ceiling.

He sat on the lavatory seat tentatively.

'Are you ready for another session?'

'OK.'

But she didn't move.

He moved his arm, shirt and all, into the water, but she smirked uneasily and sat up. With the removal of his hand she lay back.

But then she hoisted herself out of the water, and as she dried herself, he went to prepare.

He had managed, observing aspects of her face in an unusually piercing way, to shift this vision on to the canvas with a dextrous layer or two. This enlivened a modicum of gratitude, and in fact, when all was going well, he enjoyed the bonhomie of discussion.

'Oh!'

He held up his hand, she had moved too much from her position – that was better. And now he listened as she continued with her disjointed account of her dream and its meaning, apparently the outwitting of childhood assassins by means of obscure portent.

'But why do you believe that?'

There was softness to his tone that gave warning of disbelief and her enthusiasm died. The ideas conjured by its images had stimulated her – but from childhood onwards Christopher had despised this evident thrill in pattern-making – open up a sticky sheet and there you have – the stars! Not at all – just a mess of colour. It was the same for those abstract daubs of oil-paint so arbitrarily designated to represent mood, as if the very lack of representative clarity allowed this sentimental leeway. Whenever he heard fables being constructed from fragments of personal history, he would be unable to prevent this prejudice from being revealed. It would have to overrule even his infatuated indulgence towards whatever were the whims of youth.

She was chastened by his argument and after it had finished, the session continued silently. But she knew that for himself, Christopher did believe there was pattern and meaning in the stars – he believed in luck and he had every right to do so.

Chapter Thirteen

'I think you like the dog more than me!'

'More than you like him?'

'No. You know what I mean!'

Laughing and continuing to waggle the rubber toy in front of its sly face, Charles thought about Vivienne's comment. He hardly (as was the accepted wisdom) saw the dog as a less demanding object of affection – since it was a terrible nuisance much of the time, requiring the rigid routine of timetables and occasionally substitute homes during trips abroad. But he spent a great deal of time thinking about it – its comical ways. Anyway, it was a usual criticism of English men and he hadn't that much interest in the subject.

Charles got up from his game on the floor. He was bored and nowadays his boredom was emptier. It irritated him too that without responsibility had come the need for occupation, although his presence at the office could hardly be dignified under the term, necessary. In the old days he had always had work outstanding or tasks that could be put off, and then had followed the years in which the dust from the crisis was settling, enabling the state of waiting to seem normal. Back then, he could not have imagined this empty state of sanctuary to be so agitating.

He had his routine, most days he walked to the office; it took him twenty minutes. Once there, he chatted with effort to the receptionist at the main entrance. She found him sweet and liked his dog too. Then he took the cramped lift (unless there was another waiting to use it – then he would gesture to them to take it first) up to his rented office room on the third floor.

Today, Charles sat alone behind his desk and idly flicked

through an astronomy magazine that he and Laura had been looking at on the train journey back from Northumberland. What are the chances of life on other planets? It was apparently an unlikely combination of circumstances that had produced life on earth. After the initial explosion that had seared life and time into those blank spaces, the planets had come to rest in their particular orbits round the sun in exactly the right combination. Our planet's ingredients jammed together in the interminable aeons of formation, puffed out the correct mixture of carbon and oxygen. And that useless lump of dead matter, the moon, turns at exactly the right distance to balance gravity on earth. And with all these and other matter-of-fact combinations in place, then life can go through all the motions, push and probe its way out into the open – what a dull affair it is, this miracle of life!

Jake Eastman was the third partner, an American polo player without the money to pursue this sport except from the sidelines. He was older than Charles and indifferent to his greater education and sophistication. Usually arriving after lunch, he remained in the office for longest, making the transatlantic calls. The venture had been his idea and he had sold the idea to Charles one late night. In his unadventurous Virginian accent he had explored little routes to wealth, via those in America who needed contacts in England, but before the views could fully develop he would trail off. It had been tantalising enough that when Charles had found himself sitting with Paul Sikorski one night he had (perhaps with a wish to impress) furthered these possibilities – added one more layer. Paul had seen that it was a chance without any risks to himself financially, since Charles alone was providing the initial outlay. He had leant forward to hear more. Finally he had met with the two of them and had agreed to enter into it, albeit in a less active capacity. Since he had always rather disliked Paul, Charles felt all the more certain that this new partnership was fortuitous.

Nothing had happened in the four months they had been

together, but he was happy to sit in the office and Paul joined them occasionally, sitting with gloomy complaints of frustration that put Charles in the satisfactory role of optimist.

At first Charles had held back. He had not been unfaithful to Vivienne before, he was unconfident of his ability with women, and having married the most beautiful of that generation, he had rather hoped to be able to put all that effort to rest.

But something about the meeting at the Kielders' had seemed propitious. Jeanette's dullness was exactly of the sort that seemed restful, but challenging in that it was, after all, novel. Her thin face and body had the necessary ingredients to produce physical attraction, and her conversation had the pull of dead matter coming round again in compelling rhythm, as it combined with her flattering looks of admiration. And certainly he had had brewing for some time the fury produced by his own wife's romantic affairs, the sort that would propel even the most indolent into some sort of cataclysm.

And that first lunch had been easy, her sprightly manner of alighting on one subject after another – only to switch immediately to whichever subject he introduced whether it be the wine list or his work – thrilled him. She seemed nervous, but her nerves seemed so unattached to the situation that he could be flattered without any burden of responsibility.

And so, he had asked her out to lunch a few more times, had sat opposite her, roping in all his old attributes of charm that had for some time been unused. He had not been often in the testing situation of new company recently without Vivienne's presence near him, diligently rendering his own efforts obsolete, and the rediscovery of effort had filled him with a strange vigour.

He had returned to his office from the first lunch, had rung the Mayfair florist and sent her some marigolds – passing some in a street stand earlier she had exclaimed at their lovely colour, had asked teasingly if her taste was vulgar? It had become a little joke and his card had read 'not vulgar at all . . .' The three dots being quite easily conveyed to the brisk girl working in the expensive florist in question.

Then he had sat opposite the silent telephone, filled with an unaccountable certainty that one of their financial ventures would succeed against all the odds.

It had been at the third lunch that she had been the one to suggest visiting her flat – the brandies they had drunk with their coffee had given the afternoon the reckless anonymity of night-time. And at her flat, she had come into her own; her confident dealings with his initial inadequacies had grown all the more intimate with confirmation of his grateful pleasure. And the extremes to which her narrow face twisted itself, so far from its usual fluttering preoccupations, and her unusually inventive suggestions and contortions were too intriguing not to get past the guard that all his life had presented the least flattering interpretation to any daring or unusual exploit. These images sent his thoughts flying back and forth to disturbing regions that had all the appearance of being those of these hitherto closed realms of adventure.

He cleared some loose papers, put the magazine on top of them. He wondered what he could do, whom he could ring. After these few months, Charles now had the desire to confide in someone about this unlikely liaison. He wished to boast, surprise, or at least, share the humour of the situation. He had many friends, all of whom would have listened with some sympathy, but he was reluctant for male confidences. He knew that his male friends didn't quite see him in that light and so in their company he became again unworldly and uninterested in sexual chat.

Chapter Fourteen

Her grandparents had been stimulated by the flat's function-al modernity, reflected in its compact layout. The kitchen had suitably cupboard-like doors, and the long corridor led to a conveniently neat pair of bedrooms. The flat was narrow, the rooms were narrow and so were the stairs and corridor. Like a ship. Laura felt pleased. She sat on one of the beige armchairs, her hands resting on the arms. There were little flashes of familiarity in the midst of all this anonymity; the slumbering paperweight pig the colour of tomato soup and the paintings – local Scottish scenes accomplished with a flourish of abstraction (the figures had blanks instead of faces) with their plain white frames.

She got up and moved along the hall to the bedrooms. Out of the two she had picked the one looking on to the houses opposite. Now her two open suitcases lay on the floor too.

Lastly she looked into the second room. It was dark but it would be night anyway if Martin stayed over. The boxes were visible from underneath its much smaller bed, but still.

The telephone in the hall had an old-fashioned ring. She put down the broom and picked up the shiny receiver, wiped her hand down her trousers.

'Hello?'

'Hello! Where are you?'

'In the hall.'

Her father's voice seemed too improbably jolly, and she felt guilty. She had not even shared his grief, and now she was selfishly only full of distaste for the dust that had accumulated in her grandfather's wake. And so she threw herself into enthu-siasm for her flat-warming drinks gathering that evening.

'Of course you can! I need guests!'

Martin arrived early, looked around. He made a little joke about the familiarity of the bedroom curtains decorated with plums! As he tested the unyielding mattress he remembered his old room in Northumberland and the sun coming in.

'Alison's coming. And Dad briefly.'

'Vivienne?'

'No. Away.'

As she looked for a corkscrew to open his bottle of wine, he examined one or two more details of the flat, some of which brought back amused memories. On the table was a photograph. He picked it up – oh yes. It featured Hilary and Edith sitting on a garden bench in front of the low wall. Above them sat Laura and Martin, and several presents she had received for her birthday that day, as many as could cram beside her. Behind them in the distance, was the stretch of the Cheviots. Later that afternoon, the two of them had run down to continue to dig for pet creatures on the beach, the ruined abbey just visible still behind them.

She had asked, 'Do you know who lives there?'

'No.'

'God.'

He had not replied, caught off his guard.

'And do you know who owns it?'

'No.'

'We do.'

There was a ring at the doorbell. It was her father, speaking into the intercom 'It's me – well, *us*!' with girlish glee suitable for an occasion. He and his friend climbed the stairs slowly, their voices matching the pace. Evidently his friend was a woman. And at the top he presented her with pride and embarrassment shining in his face.

Jeanette said, all her words spoken with great deliberation, 'Do you remember we met at that lovely weekend?'

'Oh, yes!'

The fact that he hadn't told Laura that his friend was a

woman, and especially the woman from the Kielders' house, gave Laura grave apprehension, but she chatted to her amicably in order to appear easygoing.

Jeanette glanced round the room, saying finally, 'Oh, I do like that look before anything has been done to a place.'

She noticed Martin's polite nod.

'Oh, do you agree? I'm so glad!'

She made it quite clear by the length of her pauses that she found the task of finding topics difficult, but her occasional laugh in Charles's direction implied that this difficulty was feminine and charming. Finally they left and Laura came back aghast and amused. She sat as if exhausted, her arms out by her sides her eyes up at the ceiling.

'What the FUCK is going on!'

'I *liked* her!'

Martin's truthful riposte was lost since she was answering the door to Alison.

Chapter Fifteen

Christopher liked Laura's unorthodox stabs at conversation, he found her amusing to listen to as he worked, and he had asked that she sit tonight on her picture. That being impossible, he had had to fall back on a new drawing of a head. But it was not working and he was distracted. He remembered now that Laura had described (with, it has to be said, amusing accounts of her grandfather's spending habits) the flat into which she was moving and two old friends coming round to celebrate the fact. He had not replied to her invitation, put with rather an attractive attempt at casualness, other than to murmur 'That might be difficult . . .'

But now, unable to progress, he thought he might investigate. He clutched at his hands, but his sitter Angus Mullion remained silent.

Christopher paused at one end of the studio. Funnily enough, remembering a conversation with Laura, he had recently added a couple of crude brown lines to the bottom corner of a small work he had started at an earlier time – a little green and yellow leaf. It would never be taken further, but looking at it now, he could see that it was better for that addition. He disliked the idea of inspiration, keeping superstition at bay with the most rigorous self-denial, but he believed in taking advantage of chance.

Without work he was uneasy. Moving from one end of the room to the other, he gave a passionate defence of application over instinct and Angus remained quiet. Christopher then invited him, if he wanted to, to accompany him to a friend's flat near Hyde Park on the way to getting something to eat?

'I will, thank you.'

But his tone contained something not pleasant to Christopher's ears, a jarring note of humour so elusive a lesser man would have missed it.

Christopher left the room in such a manner that it was incumbent on Angus to follow. In the kitchen Christopher put on his coat, and then returned to the studio room, wrapped the unfinished canvas in brown paper and they left the flat.

Christopher found it hard to let go of his friendships, since often the nature of the break was extreme and irrevocable. They drove along in silence. Angus had been in his life for many years but recently the highly strung nature of his personality that had seemed once to produce such originality, now seemed only to bring forth bitterness. Angus was conscious of this but could or would not alter the downward spiral.

Since the publication of his novel *Champagne and Wine* over a decade earlier, Angus had not attempted another book. Christopher had read this novel admiringly at proof stage, before the cult status had formed that might or might not have put him off its amusing little turns of phrase. He had not taken amiss the veiled account of their brief physical affair since it had been portrayed in the spirit with which it had taken place, as a manifestation of the wayward spirit of the times. In his subtler days, Angus had recognised that Christopher's admiration or affection often took the form of sexual attraction, and it was only nowadays, aged thirty-eight and bitter, that he confided his opinion of Christopher's suppressed homosexuality, apparent in his sexual disgust ('. . . and can we blame him?') for women. It might have been thought that this would be a sympathetic revelation, but being based on a fabrication, it wasn't.

Christopher was dismayed by Angus's lack of discipline, uncharacteristically had been recently moved to venture the mild reproof, 'If you're a writer, you have to write surely?'

But drunkenness had all but smothered the sparks ignited from the combat with failure and he had answered sneeringly, 'We haven't all got your European work ethic.'

The recurrent smell of stale alcohol could have been tolerated, but his manner that had once been so admirably unpredictable now on several instances seemed repulsive, the insolent nature of his comments, not daring but tiresome.

They had been discussing Mrs Ruth. Laura was still laughing as she answered the doorbell, surprise in her voice – but the small, unlikely 'hello?' filled her with triumph and dismay. She pressed the buzzer and thought to warn her guests – she took one step as if to do so, but turned back, hovering in agitation by the door as the steps drew slowly nearer. As he came through the door, Christopher introduced Angus, who greeted her with a bright smile, then waited for Christopher's clasp to end and the three of them went into the room.

Alison at least had vulgarity enough not to be altogether repelled by the unorthodox, although she had rarely encountered it in its true form. But the old man creeping into the room could not enter her sexual frame of reference. She didn't know anything about him, but she knew enough to recognise the aura of fame, all of them in the room did, jerked and immobilised by its electric charge. Christopher nodded his hello to each in turn, introduced his guest in a murmur and answered Laura's politely laughing 'Drink?' by thrusting the little gift into her hand, the one that was still discreetly pushing his away.

Angus took his offered glass, and his smile still in place, moved to sit in the small chair in the corner of the room. He hardly needed to look around; his malicious tendencies prevented that little courtesy. But he was somewhat amused by the impressions that he had assembled on his journey to the chair, of the complete lack of elegance in the room. He had not seen the like since having left his parental home in Aberdeen at a young age – he had put his parents' disinterest in decorative embellishment down to working-class indifference and exhaustion – but here it was again.

She was asking, 'Have you got a drink?'

He raised his glass and nodded his head, his smile fixed and relentlessly non-committal.

It was intolerable, the atmosphere! Laura called Alison over to look at the present. She was glad to move since Christopher had sat himself down by her side, leaning over to examine the photograph on the table with an act of casualness.

'How lovely!'

Christopher's works could almost be said to be intriguing representatives of that artistic thin line between genius and vulgar incompetence. Certainly, as Alison examined the little gift, she would have slid it into the latter category. It was all little drawings and patches of green and yellow, representing a jungle? No, a sort of plant. And at its foot, a whiskery little smear of brown paint – a creature?

The chat continued and none of the talk was remotely interesting. Laura could tell that. Nor did it have the ease of familiarity. She told them about the job she was soon to start, in a design shop. They hadn't heard of it, no. And Martin's laugh that might have led to hilarity at her unlikely choice, went nowhere. In the silence, Alison told Laura that her father had a new book of poetry just out.

Christopher's stillness grew more contorted still.

At first he had thought the way Alison carried her unworldly bulk was admirable, as if sliding round the subject. But now listening to her enthusiastic flippancy concerning this book, he found his interest dissolving, a residue of disgust the only remains.

Finally he murmured, 'I'm going to have to go . . .'

And he left as he always did, vaguely but with purpose, his eyes on the door warily as if invisibly shadowing an important forerunner. Angus left too, turning back to give a smile of thanks, its brilliance again leaving a shiver of humiliation in Laura's heart.

Then they were left to themselves, flat and relieved without their demanding presence.

Chapter Sixteen

Laura felt shamefully, that it could never be said that she made no effort to make friends. Her new job in the modern design shop had thrown her into a merry new crowd and at first the fact that they didn't despise her made her think they liked her. The truth was, they weren't interested in her at all. Tonight, this became obvious by the second bar – Ralph, the joker of the gang, was animatedly telling a risqué anecdote and turned to gesticulate a part of the story, his animated back remained for too long in Laura's view for her participatory smile to remain in place.

She turned and saw that a man was staring at her, the boredom of his expression mismatched by his latent intensity. His one gold ear-stud looked disconcerting, he must have been nearly forty. But his face had the vivid glow of one famous and she blushed. Then she remembered she'd met him with Christopher. She raised her hand casually and he at once turned away. But it was too late for dissimulation and she continued towards him and his group of companions at the far end of the bar.

'Oh *that* painting – you know – that night in my flat – I thought I'd seen your face before!'

'Not only his face . . .'

At Angus's gloomy expression, she laughed uproariously, folding herself over him in hilarity. Normally Angus disliked the intimacy of young girls but that night she had inadvertently charmed him. Having observed her overdressed appearance from his corner of the French pub all those many months back, he had been prepared for middle-class quirkiness, not outright social imbecility; his writer's instincts had been awoken by her shamefaced struggles from her beige chair.

He could see she was making quite a hit with this company, especially two Hurst sisters, Catherine and Isobel, and their Welsh cousin Gareth, who with the last round of drinks was gently declining towards an onlooker's sorrow. They were a few years older than she was but they knew her name – their parents knowing hers, had discussed the affair with Christopher. But it was clear that they had none of the prudery of their parents' generation – far from it! They asked questions of the intrusive sort that would sustain the mood of hilarity.

Following one, Catherine turned to Angus, 'And . . . didn't you also have some sort of romantic get-together . . . ?'

'Oh not for years.'

He didn't add his usual gross witticism on the nature of the 'famous artist's' drooping physique, an addition with which he enlivened most productions of the story. His listeners were rarely averse to hearing insults of that nature directed towards Christopher or anyone else, but Angus was still sober enough to understand that it might be an unpalatable indication of Christopher's heterosexuality. Instead, he raised his glass to Laura with casual malice.

'So – to new friends. Bottoms up!'

PART III

Chapter Seventeen

Two years after they'd first met and Christopher was in love with Laura. This particular and unlikely prediction, made to herself before she'd even met the man, was now fulfilled. And the magnificent scale of these early romantic dreams (constructed with a most timid attention to detail) was quite lived up to in the extent of his anguish now at any signs of disinterest on her part.

One afternoon after work, having picked her up in his van, he offered her five hundred pounds to leave her job, with assurances that modelling for him would be a proper occupation. Laura hesitated at first. The thick bundle of notes pushed towards her seemed a dirty intrusion into her picture of romantic success. She spoke a little of what she understood to be embarrassment as he ducked his head away. But later in private, pulling these same notes out of her pocket, their extraordinary abundance seemed to suggest a more sustained freedom than a mere keepsake would have provided.

And so, from having required nothing from him, not time, affection, commitment nor even conversation, Laura now began to demand everything including and most especially, money. And the last being the easiest, he was happy to provide it in great wads as was always his habit in romance.

And they went on outings – to the Zoo after hours where he had been given permission to paint Simurgh the elephant. All through the paths, he kept up his writhing embraces, behind the disapproving and silent back of the Zoo manager leading the way.

Christopher whispered with erotic intimacy, 'Do you like elephants?'

'They're all right.'

And Christopher laughed with delight at her eccentric reservations.

Clasping her to him, he asked in another whisper, 'What do you like then?'

She couldn't help but laugh.

'Amphibians.'

The manager, Mr Aiselbie, turned then, with a guarded look. 'Amphibians did you say? Then – perhaps . . . ?'

They pushed past him and he allowed the door to close, his authority back in the darkness.

And they moved from case to case, watching the creatures inch themselves about, as at home now as the plants they moved about in. She had announced her preference in a moment of flippancy, but now she liked watching them going about their business and making the best of their limited habitats. The frog flattened against the glass was comical and disgusting. Its blank expression was amusing, its flabby flesh rendered more colourless still with this unseemly pressure.

'You know they say in that poem, animals don't get resentful?'

No one replied, so she continued, 'But they do. Our dog used to sulk if we went away on holiday without him.'

'I don't read much poetry.'

But still the room presented little fragments of primeval life and it was most interesting.

Something about the evening had displeased Mr Aiselbie. Back in his office, he returned the chairs to their correct places. Images of unsettling eroticism were swilling around.

He had received his first curious letter asking that Christopher be allowed to paint the elephant in privacy over a year ago. He had found its lack of information rather exciting. He had made some enquiries; although he had heard of the name, he had little else to go on. But with a rare burst of perversity, the pursed look of fascinated disapproval on a colleague's face had decided him. He had interpreted the look as coming from envy. He had written back and the painting sessions had started.

Their little ritual was that they meet at the gate and walk together to the enclosure. Occasionally Simurgh would need to be coaxed and shoved back into her normal position. After a few hours, he would return and Christopher and he would walk back together then have a coffee in his office.

But today Mr Aiselbie felt that he had been witness to the less agreeable aspect of notoriety. The girl was young enough to be Christopher's granddaughter. And the man seemed to lose his aloof dignity in her presence, pushing himself against her like that with grovelling sprightliness. This discourtesy had continued even throughout the casually requested explanation – Simurgh, the bird of realisation, carrying up the nine elephants, symbols of dense matter in Indian creation myth.

Mr Aiselbie was sophisticated. He disliked having to shift to the ranks of the disapproving, but nevertheless, it now was happening. He marked the next meeting Christopher had requested, circling the date on his wall calendar with a red pen, then allowed the front pages to flap back into place.

Chapter Eighteen

Charles and Vivienne's life together was growing unhealthily sodden and bleak. Their marriage had always had a certain admirable flourish to it, not to everyone's taste, but it could be seen that their chat was always animated and their social life varied and humorous. But with this aspect neglected, the unpleasant realities were gaining sodden ground, the financial depreciation and the hitherto unspoken resentments.

Even now, they still felt the loss of Kentigern as a bond, believing that such a magnificent scale of loss must, at some point, provide some compensatory glory. But as the years drew on, the money grew less and even the scaled-down vision of an additional country house (the modesty of which plan had given Vivienne pride) looked increasingly unlikely. If the subject was broached, Charles looked evasive, and even occasionally allowed his impatience to show. Vivienne had always prided herself on her pragmatism; she often alluded to it in wry comparison to her husband's dreaming and spending. Not the least of her fury was the role she was being fitted into, that of the unrealistic extravagant.

All during the upheaval Vivienne had pulled herself into performing supportively, and her stoicism had suited Charles's desire for evasion. But now she was beginning to regret her silent fatalism, and to make up for it referred back spitefully to that family loss on many occasions. Their chat was still animated, but without its foundation of affection or hope, it grew up in desperate exaggerated tendrils, each more feeble and unpleasant to the spectator.

Charles's romance should have balanced the scales that had been upset by Vivienne's dalliances, all of which had taken place in the far-off days when there was enough space for privacy. But increasingly he looked at her with something like hatred, remembering her disloyalty. And in spite of his own secret life, the more her face twisted into unattractive dissatisfaction and misery, the more he loathed her for her one-time frivolous affairs.

He knew that it had almost come to the point where a decision would have to be made, an admission too. The questions were getting more pointed. The other day Vivienne had asked about his late return home and had started crying about the Christmas preparations that were looming and left for she alone to arrange. Her demands were increasing with every month that went by, she needed money and reassurance in equally impossible quantities. Now even Charles, like an obdurate beachcomber, had to concede to the mounting storm; battered and spat at by its elements, soon it would be impossible to ignore it altogether. Now he pulled himself together.

'I'm only away a week – why don't you ring Laura, meet up with her?'

'Her paramour too, I suppose.'

'Why not?'

Laura was flattered by Vivienne's playful request for entertainment, mistaking her tone for camaraderie. Having put down the telephone, she suggested to Christopher that 'The Club' was the place to take her – expensive and grand.

Once they were sat at their table, Vivienne flirted with tactlessness – archly referring to Christopher's clandestine romances, in the clipped manner of the just. She felt herself to be on the side of righteousness, after all. Evidently he did not feel the same; he looked away in boredom. But his silence had not caused Vivienne any hesitation. When Laura brought up the subject of Edward Kielder's visions, an attempt at a safe topic, Vivienne used it as a springboard to launch herself further into Christopher's private life.

She had been drunk and looked old. Her eyes were pulled

down with self-pity. This look, so far from her usual elegance, might have been thought to have appealed to Christopher, accused so often of relishing disintegration and representing it as truth, but it did not. Indeed he could hardly look at her.

He had in earlier years, admired her beauty and elegance in clinical manner but it was not of the sort to appeal to him even then. Somehow it seemed constructed from bits and pieces artfully compiled, but the whole wasn't there. He preferred a whole even if it consisted of inferior basic material, and he admired mess.

Jane rarely visited her husband's club, but tonight she couldn't resist witnessing Christopher's little family outing. In recent months it had become clear from the way that he talked of her, that his liking for Laura had transformed into infatuation. This happened from time to time and usually passed, but she was curious to see how this light of love would manifest on such unfavourable ground.

As she approached the awkward group, sitting in front of their 'exquisite nursery delicacies' she started to laugh. Christopher on seeing her, lit up too – he quite understood the nature of her amusement.

He moved to let her in and Vivienne started immediately on a lively disparagement of their husbands' joint business venture.

Jane threw up her hands. 'Oh, don't tell me!'

Looking at Laura's polite smile, she added in a humorous undertone, 'How can I put this – if Charles is involved, it's bound to fail.'

Vivienne understood this to be an affectionate compliment towards an old friend, a joke of the sort she would never be able to pull off – though God knows, she tried.

They ordered puddings and Laura remained silent, smiling when appropriate. She appeared infantile in this company, sipping the expensive burgundy like a precocious delinquent.

Jane hardly felt it was her duty to nurse her along, but now she included her. 'Paul's got another plan in the pipeline – a Scottish club – I hope you'll go when it eventually opens – I'm sure it could do with some youthful blood.'

She couldn't help but feel for her – there in the presence of her dreadful mother. In the last year, they had met a few times and Laura had made some efforts to please, knowing how much Jane was part of Christopher's life. Now Laura had less wish to please on that account, but there was another.

She said, 'Your nephew Tom is coming to a lecture at Queensgate tomorrow – on metaphysics.'

'Oh God! He's obviously got more of my brother's blood than I thought . . .'

Though willing to continue the joke, Jane had to go. She left briskly, waving a distant hand – she rather disliked all the business of lengthy goodbyes.

Vivienne said that she too must leave. As she thanked Christopher, she bit her lip and looked angrily ready to cry. Why? What did she want? Reassurance? Money?

Laura continued to drink and Christopher mused.

'The thing about your mother' (he lowered his voice to make his point) 'she has the artfulness of a child who has been spoilt by some grotesque act committed *as a child* . . .'

As far as Laura knew, Vivienne had committed no acts of a disgusting nature as a child, beyond what is entirely usual, but he persisted in his argument. And all the while, his considerable abilities that should have led him straight to the correct conclusions, were hampered and knocked aside by his strangely dogged pursuit of the least promising, the least attractive line. Certainly least attractive to the subjects concerned, often containing one or two penetrating truisms and many more that sounded appallingly likely even if not actually true at all. And hardly attractive to the world at large unless directed to the growing band of admirers, who took his delight in spitefully obscure fault-finding to their hearts and minds, as chosen guardians of his privilege.

In a moment's silence, Laura suggested they dance. She

thought that she would regain the advantage on the dance floor, even though the hits from the ruder discos were disinfected on this neat green square of glass. And she would have been correct, but for Christopher's lewd moves that destroyed her rhythm. Her bump and grind that had some abandonment were reduced to agonised twitchings as she risked pushing his hand away, with a polite laugh. He pulled her to him and held her close as they meandered round the small space to the song about starmen.

'In relation to number one, number two is the potential for expression and manifestation. Because it is not itself manifest, it appears to be hidden. The blueprint for this leaf is expressed in numerical form . . .'

Throughout the hour-long talk – the agreeably harmonious numbers that added up to proof of a divine order in the universe, Laura listened to every third sentence. The rest of the time, her thoughts sat with the couple behind her – Tom and his girlfriend Molly.

At its conclusion, she was easily able to turn to Angus and say musingly, 'Interesting . . .'

'Come on – he's at the front.'

It wasn't always sexual attraction that dictated Angus's enthusiasms. In this case, it was. He had met Abed in the French pub, and had listened to his convoluted arguments that more or less followed the line of tonight's lecture, the second in a series. Although Abed had urged attendance, he now looked a bit embarrassed to see them all there, since he was with a friend. But he was naturally convivial and his friend too seemed willing to go for the suggested drink at the pub round the corner. As the talk went on, the curiosity of the moon being so perfectly placed, the similarly accomplished dimensions of the earth . . . Laura listened to Tom's occasional interjection – his absolute lack of humour was a source of glamour. After a while, she went to call Christopher as she'd promised to do. Coming back, she announced that he was going to join them. Abed expressed the view that being a painter he would know about all this stuff. He had with him a book that linked dreaming and creativity and brought it out to show them.

When Christopher arrived they moved to make room for him and Abed, notes from the lecture to hand, continued the conversation, saying, 'I don't believe in God in the religious sense, but the symmetry of design must mean some creator at work surely?'

'No.'

But Abed, looking back at his notes, persisted, 'But you must admit, the anthropic principles here, must suggest consciousness over coincidence?'

'No such thing. Why should anything have a meaning?'

'No, no – come on! Your paintings have meaning, don't they?'

Tom leered round with imbecilic triumph and it was only for the glamour of his youth that Christopher answered him at all.

'They don't have any meaning over and above what they are.'

Chapter Nineteen

Laura knew Christopher to be of the old school. Not only was he old himself, but his tendencies were towards those sensibilities of a previous generation. He held privacy to be of the utmost importance, going to any lengths to secure it. He despised the need to discuss such lengths, seeing protestation in this case as evidence of modern mediocrity and half-heartedness. Privacy as everyone knows, is a statement of artistic or religious intent; but could he just not, like most of the celebrated, let in a little acclaim to flavour those dull times of solitude? But Laura had enough taste to appreciate such authenticity. She admired in her heart, his circuitous other lives, all around but hidden from her.

Sitting in his van as he sidled off to visit a flat behind Baker Street ('just for a minute') she imagined a few goings on within the rooms up there, of an amorous nature she assumed. But her mind soon moved on to livelier topics and the subject that gave her most interest was that of her new popularity with – and again, it buoyed her up to remember this – the sorts of friends who found her passions and humour similar to their own. Perhaps it was the fact that their childhoods had been so like hers – it was the sort of friendship she had not experienced before. She felt at ease enough with them to be able to joke about anything, especially some of the more extreme aspects of nursery life. But, superstitiously, she refrained from mentioning the abusive incident on the beach. Nowadays she had a fear that the undignified nature of this introduction, which might have affected her sexual allure, infected her in some way with its unsavoury aspects, and she thought it better to keep it quiet. Certainly she never had much success in that field from her contemporaries and it was a failure that she still often dwelt on. But for now at least, the very notorious nature of her romance with Christopher – if too peculiar to indicate a definite verdict on her sex appeal – could be taken to be romantic at least.

She looked up at the window.

The night before she had had a gathering at her flat, consisting of Catherine, her younger sister, Isobel, and her comically churlish boyfriend Ray. And Tom – and, of course, the initial instigator of this new milieu – Angus.

Christopher's shadow appeared at the window, froze ambiguously and then moved on.

And these new friends had found her flat hilarious, Catherine especially appreciated the lack of any change of homely touch (seeing straight through the practical sounds Laura had made about money and needing time to live in it and such like). Instead, she had at once swivelled the rustic landscapes straight with appreciative amusement, the more unequivocal Ray at her side, grunting with flattering disbelief. They all had appraised the little present from Christopher up on the mantelpiece with raised eyebrows and pursed lips.

'Mmm, very nice, very nice indeed, my girl! Hello!' (Pointing to the little whiskered creature unformed in one corner.)

And they had slumped down in the beige armchairs and had returned to the ever-delightful subject explored even on the first night they'd met – Edward Kielder's ghosts. Tom alone was not amused by his father's visitations, but he hid his indifference so as not to be thought priggish.

'From outer space or his unconscious?'

'If outer space – why did they pick him for a view of human life?'

They saw no reason to doubt the ambiguous; God himself could have appeared and they would have taken Him in their stride. All they asked for was that their time be uneven enough to be amusing. And they could and did sit for hours, discussing such and more personal matters – Laura's affair and its humorous offshoots – Mr Aiselbie, and his exhausting attempts to please his celebrated visitor (the wretched elephant wouldn't budge).

Apparently they had affection for fame and what of it? It may be an abhorrent side-effect of genius – but most people do want a little acclaim for their efforts. Authenticity is usually just as repulsive after a while, since it is after all, unusual. And, increasingly, Christopher's strange little turns of phrase, signifying an anguished tenderness, had begun to illustrate his inadequacies. The great age that distanced him from the humour of her generation, the physical movements of distress occasioned by her indifference to his wheedling words and the general foreignness of his tastes and allusions, all of these left Laura impatient and revolted.

And here he was, opening the car door without even her noticing his return. He sat down in the driver's seat, but made no move to start the car.

'Would you mind if I got you a taxi? I may have to stay here for a while.'

Laura did mind, because her day had been planned out. Now she would have to think of something to do on her own. It was Saturday, and what the hell was there to do? He saw her sullen face, but had already slid towards her hand.

'Something towards the taxi . . . '

Readjusting her features took some effort, but she managed it.

'OK. That's fine. Don't worry, it's fine.'

'Will I see you later?'

'Yes, I'll come round.'

And in the taxi, she went through the notes. Quite enough.

Later that night she came round, full of chemically induced enthusiasm. Christopher watched her pace around and his heart that pounded ruthlessly with evolutionary supremacy, whose terrible force gained him entry into whatever situation that his mind toyed with, now grew sluggish with gloom.

On her way out of the room, she turned to ask, 'Do you want some?'

'No.'

Cocaine was not to his taste, but he knew it to be the drug of sex. Her answer to his careful 'Do you have to take that stuff?' was 'It's normal enough.' And increasingly, it seemed that for Laura, it was.

Returning from the bathroom, she appeared to have the gleam of erotic fanaticism in her eyes, although they were not blazoning in his direction, but around the room as she spoke of her latest plan – of collaborating with Angus in turning his novel into a film script. It had been put forward as a casual suggestion that night – that his book should be made into a film by a friend of Catherine's who had recently produced a feature film and had had some success with it. This man had been laconic in regard to detail (he hadn't read the novel) but others in the group had chivvied the idea along. As the drinks had flowed and the awareness of its cult status had materialised, he had become more definite – he had proposed a meeting with his partner at which an option could be discussed. And the name – perhaps too suggestive of the unpopular world of privilege . . . Anyway, that could be decided later – he had suggested a first draft – or an outline then? (Even he could not have missed the grimace on Angus's face at the prospect of these speculative pages.)

But Laura was entranced – she certainly had an affinity with drunkenness! And from her recent expeditions with Angus, she knew the allure of the Soho daytime drinking world – a closed fairground, broken into, its idle amusements to be lolled over – this atmospheric world, so effectively evoked in his novel, must be conveyed on the screen!

She could hardly have missed Christopher's gloom and asked, 'Do you think I'm incapable?'

'Oh, I think you could do it – but after all, what is there to do?'

Christopher's reluctance remained; it wasn't even that he

didn't consider a film script to be worthy of much interest – but recently her mentions of Angus's name had increased in frequency and enthusiasm, commensurate with his own growing desires to avoid it altogether.

He would never fall into the lazy old ways of putting up with the unacceptable behaviour of friends for longer than was logical. Yes, she understood it to be another of his courageous stances against the pleasant dullness of habit.

Chapter Twenty

The amoebic shapes on the ceiling merged and separated with slow grace. But the angular black shadow was intruding and Charles brought his eyes down to this flapping evidence – the florist's bill. He was sodden with drink and resentment of the worst sort, the triumphant sort. Vivienne stared at him, her shrill enquiries uselessly petering off his unbecoming defences. In answer to the last question, he lifted his face into a frightful caricature of fatalism.

'I can only say – it just happened.'

She stared some more at his grey woollen jersey.

'It didn't – JUST HAPPEN.'

She was off again.

'And *her* . . . ?'

Eventually he produced the appallingly dignified, 'I think it might be better if I stay at my club tonight.'

As the front door closed, Vivienne felt overpowering relief. She sank into a chair and chided herself immediately back to the correct mood with tales of the injustice having been done to her. She stared at the room that she had created; it now had the cheap shine of failure to it. Each aspect or object was expensive and desirable, but the overall image that once had seemed satisfactory now swam away again from her view.

She was aghast. That was the only word. For so long she had felt every justification in drinking, demanding presents and picking arguments about every innocent grievance, all in some misty unshaped belief that there was something to blame him for, something that was causing her suffering or about to. She had assumed – God knows she hadn't examined the question further, absorbed in her drunken recriminatory miasma – that it would remain thus until some violent occurrence perhaps blew the whole situation apart, leaving her, as she had admirably proven capable of, squaring up to disaster.

But this woman! It was inconceivable, a humiliatingly bad joke. During the recent months, she had pondered the possibility of unfaithfulness certainly, but had rejected in all seriousness the scenario of another woman. His mood had been so spoilt and resentful, drunken and bored. Each night his eyes had remained balefully on hers until drifting back to the ceiling, the eternal indicator of pointlessness.

Why did he hate her so much? Oh – she horrified him. Her brisk footsteps and nervous head movements, her bracelets jingling as her animated responses increased. Charles sat in the taxi, his head ponderously following the turns as he returned the driver's chat, clutching the handle to prevent slipping.

Yes, her snobbery too. Not the snobbery itself – since after all, quite a compliment to him – but its manifesting in all the interminable invitations they had to accept, and all sorts of charm that he had to witness and to some extent join in with. And her audience always laughing and taken with her efforts, taken with her, and he despised them for it. And her infidelities? Those betrayals had dug too deep into his soul to be a feasible source of hatred; wrenching them up now to brood over would have uprooted other humiliations and so he preferred to look to the smaller crimes to do the job of justification.

Had any members of his club been of the observant sort, they would have seen a gleam in Charles's eye that might have suggested a wish to confide. But at that hour, even if such members did exist, they were elsewhere and there was a mood of somnolence. But embarking on an adventure of such magnitude, Charles could not help but feel lively.

He walked towards the telephone, situated on a round table in the hall, and sat on the chair beside it, flipping the telephone directory in an attempt to gather his thoughts. What previous words of tenderness had he used to alert

Jeanette to her imminent new status? In truth, he had thought to leap into the stormy seas without warning – then, should terror have forced him to retreat at the last minute, no one would have known of his indecision and cowardice.

He picked up the receiver and dialled, but at the first ring, he froze – how was he to put it? He almost hung up – but it was answered and too late he had asked, 'Hello?'

At the other end, Jeanette knew at once that this was the moment that she had wanted for some time. Even such as she had social arts and she had allowed him to indulge for many months in the absolute exhaustion of the fed-up, his head resting back on the chair as he brooded on marital weariness.

As he listened to her talk, did he even approach the little thought that sparked in some corner of his brain – that the words of welcome lacked the warmth of originality? No, he relied on the comforting conclusion, that now she could take over and he could relax. He had done enough and thought enough.

And in his quest for a buried and safe life, he had refused to dig out the unpalatable possibility that he might now be merely substituting one sort of hard work for another. He felt as if he were moving to a cosier reality, as if replacing a charismatic but insincere high-ranking post for a lower, more meaningful one. Now, in the glamour of the decision, he could not see all the tiresome bureaucracy that would land on his hands, tasks that previously he had been quite able to delegate.

Jeanette might not demand social advancement, nor an extravagant lifestyle. But she would witness their absence in a most dismal manner, looking out as if through his eyes with suppressed but evident amazement. He had had no experience of this sort of woman, had no idea that a sparse imagination would place such demands on him. He would have to provide what little vision was needed, and even that little was a great deal for one such as he. All this he might have intuited, had he listened to the hints and intimations from

113

recent times, the party at which she had stood, her obscure facial expressions implying apparently disbelief that no one rushed to stand with them. The television programme at which her laughter had joined his a minute late each time, as if incredulity was the prompt; her lack of confidence never manifested in an urge for the absurd.

But still, during the journey there, he was sustained by the thrill of decision. And as the taxi drew to a halt in the narrow street, and her door opened eagerly at its sound, if her open arms and pleased expression could not be confused for glamour it was, after all, marvellously sweet, her grabbing of his hand, the squeeze and the pull towards the inside of her flat.

'Oh, how lovely to see you!'

He knew in his heart he was being lazy, but he felt he had quite enough on his plate already, without the heightened emotions of love. Change itself was enough to enliven him and the dish set before him was bland and comforting. And who is to say that they are any the wiser, who surprise their palate with little delicacies of a most surprising and peculiar nature, every mouthful demanding interest?

Chapter Twenty-one

It took a great deal longer for Angus to find his invitation in his jacket than the elderly couple behind him had bargained for. With the courtesy of an older generation, they had politely stood aside when he and Laura had marched ahead towards the official collecting names at the gates. But it was irritating after a while, the haphazard manner of his search. It was holding up not only the two of them, but also the growing number of other guests behind them, cold in the Scottish evening air.

Finally Laura asked, 'Have you *lost* the goddamned invitation?'

'That – would hardly be a fucking *tragedy*.'

He had removed his tie ceremoniously for this pronouncement, losing further precious minutes that could have been better spent. But finally the invitation was found, and they were allowed up the roped-off stairs that led to the club.

'Glad you came?'

'No.'

Once inside, the hall was as cavernous as a nave. The mirrors reflected severely; they were so grand they could afford to be frivolous in shape. It was a neo-classical Edinburgh town house that had lain empty for some years, and for the last two Paul Sikorski had been converting it into a dining club while ensuring that its original charm was retained. Its American owner had kept it pristine, the floors shone dully, the old wood had been polished, but its contents had lost their liveliness by not being used. Over in one corner, Paul held court in his usual manner, silently, with a weary smile on his face, his eyes trailing round lazily, not missing a thing. As ever, Jane stood by her husband's side, more animated but not less forbidding in her sarcastic boredom.

Jane had had some input as to her husband's guest list, compiled some months back. Following a request from Christopher she had added Laura's name, though the act of writing it for Paul's secretary brought to her mind the sight of her at a recent party and she had felt irritated anew. In spite of Laura's animation, it had almost seemed that the glow of youth that so often renders dissipation charming was transforming prematurely into something less forgivable.

Jane had insisted to Paul that Charles, too, be invited. This last, having a moral dimension, she had needed to bring to his attention personally. He had concurred.

Their modest business venture together was not doing well and Paul neither blamed Charles nor felt guilty for the latter's losses. Paul was not a romantic and did not believe that this particular business would turn the corner at this late stage, but he had been too busy recently to deal with it in any form.

But Charles's voice on the telephone, expressing regret at his inability to attend, and his shy expression of pleasure at the thought of eating there some time after the opening party, had reminded Paul of his genuine charm. They had had a little laugh together at the inconclusive nature of the recent business offensive.

When Jane saw his laughter, she had mouthed 'Charles?' And on his nod had seized the phone.

'You don't want to make an effort to come to this' – she muffled herself against the phone incompetently – '*Goddawful* party – is that right? Now come on – we all have to make an effort sometimes.'

Charles had been delighted at the other end – giggling and denying her accusations – protesting the necessity of his having to be in London at that particular time.

'Yes, *yes*! I'm sure! So – is marriage on the cards?'

'I think so.'

'Are we going to be allowed to meet her . . . ?'

'I'd love that.'

'Good!'

After a bit more chat, Charles had replaced the phone, his face shining with the reminder of the agitating old days of popularity.

Much as he held it back wearily, talking to his uncle across the room, Tom's dark hair always fell back into the geometric lines of a cartoon character's – perhaps a swot's?

Laura saw that Angus was following her gaze and she turned back to him casually. 'I don't hold out much hope for this party. What does Tom's expression indicate – boredom?'

'Or perhaps – stupidity?'

Laura blushed, answering with half-hearted defiance, 'He's hardly stupid – he has original ideas.'

'O-rigi – O-Christ!'

Seeing them looking his way, Tom came up – he greeted Angus with as much enthusiasm as he ever allowed himself. He looked Laura up and down. He always seemed to find it hard to think of things to say to her.

'Are you staying at a hotel?'

'Yes.'

'You should have stopped off at our house on the way up. It has some funny things in it. It might have given you inspiration!'

Laura blushed, that Angus's eyes were on her – so many times had she thrown in stories of childhood visits, of being, really, part of the family.

'I have stayed there already.'

But Tom's eyes, when they were alert, went directly towards Angus otherwise drifted around the rest of the room. After a moment he left to greet a friend who had just arrived.

Angus and Laura wandered along to get a drink. He said in desultory manner, 'Doesn't his indifference mean he finds you attractive? That's as I understand the sexual machinations of heterosexuals.'

That heartened Laura only slightly, and as she walked and

117

made bright sarcastic conversation to all and sundry, the chemicals of alcohol swirled horribly against those of failure. For the last few months, she seemed to have shifted from her position, she noticed that her drunken hopelessness occasionally produced looks of irritation – as if even with this tolerant crowd, she had gone one enthusiastic step too far.

For a while she paused, standing and listening to Angus talk to two old queens about gentlemen's clubs. She had last had dinner with her father and Jeanette only a week ago in their new home in Putney. Whenever she saw her father she spoke of those in her circles, many of whom he knew as children of old friends, and his face would grow sulky and guarded. He would look to Jeanette, whose face would be tight and impatient too, as if in the presence of a child naughtily dribbling. But why settle for less than the original? Why give up social aspirations? Her friends structured the world for her. If one or more were offhand, she could only assume that her worth was less overall, for who could imagine that the opinion in question was one in isolation? They formed her picture of the world; their removal left its layout in ruins. So if one of her friends were rude or dismissive, they had still to be re-conquered or she had to sit and contemplate this failure.

She nudged Angus's elbow and he turned with a look of affront at the interruption.

'I'm just going for a pee.'

'Yes, well, don't worry, dear, I think I can manage without you for a bit.'

The lavatory had a mirror inside its locked door and she was able to look at herself without interference. She was thinner, but her face had a shine of sweat. Cold, but she was always cold.

She undid the packet now. It was quite full, but she separated just enough of the brown powder, then a fraction more. She was careless, some of it fell on the floor and she left it there. Closing and wrapping up the packet first, she sniffed up her one line with the satisfaction of restraint. She sat on the closed lid of the loo, and waited for the inroads through the channels of her bloodstream and brain, past the customary disturbance with the already present alcohol.

The rush of cocaine was all very well, but increasingly, its effects had only added to the agitation of alcohol and of the amphetamine pills taken to curb her appetite. In her teenage days, she had smoked a few joints with Alison and those she had not properly inhaled; the effects had been a stimulation of her sense of daring alone. But try as she would nowadays more thoroughly to access its alleged calming benefits, she disliked that heavy uncontrolled weight in her solar plexus that would erupt into the runaway laughter of a lunatic strapped down and unable to stop.

But of heroin, the most obvious and since confirmed, the most effective source of tranquillity, she had always been superstitiously afraid. She had believed all the cautionary tales she had read and heard. The mysterious allure of the dark dripping cave – were those jewels ahead? Tiptoeing up (Oh, why not) and then bang – down into its inescapable pit and its jewels were just the gleam of the dragon's eyes.

She looked in the mirror again.

No, she had had to overcome various terrors in order to get as far as she had with this drug that still featured so heavily in underground literature and folklore. The first time didn't count; she had taken it by accident thinking it to be cocaine. Thereafter, in the midst of the party that was going on, she had gone to sleep and had woken surprisingly unembarrassed to find herself on a strange sofa, having slept for an hour. Later, she had had to wonder if it had been the guiltless nature of the encounter that had allowed her to escape the consequences. However, she couldn't avoid the fact that her system had been exposed once without calamity. After some time and hesitation, she decided to return to the same source and ask for it deliberately. That second time, over her trepidation, she had been amazed at the subtle confidence that had settled like a heavy and reassuring weight. Now that weight remained, but irritation too, an added layer.

Tomorrow she and Angus were off to stay in another part of Edinburgh, she to stay with Martin, Angus to be put up in another hotel. As part of a forthcoming pre-summer festival, he had been invited to be part of a literary reading – whose creative theme 'heroes and drunkards' allowed him access.

He had no enthusiasm for the task, it had hardly been hidden, that he was far down the list of desired and more recent authors. But boredom and the thought of selling some copies of his book gave him a con man's temporary vivacity. Laura had suggested she accompany him and he had not demurred, nor at arriving a day early to take in this party. During their travels, she had said, they could discuss the film idea further – (though 'further' was too generous a description, since Angus had been unwilling to discuss the idea at all during the six months since it had first been proposed). In the presence of his silence, her inspiration shrivelled up, but she wrote ideas, many of them, in the privacy of her notebook. At one point she had showed him a selection of these notes – they were fairly original – but originality alone? He had been able to be pleasant, looking out of the train window on the trip up. The novel opened in Edinburgh – so for research purposes – 'research!' Angus had listened for long enough. He knew enough to understand her enthusiasm, but he could not stand that word – the self-indulgent steps of creative self-help enthusiasts.

Laura came out of the cubicle, stood in front of the basins. Her face glowed again. The connecting door opened and the noise of the party roared in. Did she want to face the crowds again? Did she fuck.

'Excuse me . . .'

Without looking at her, Laura pushed herself against the basin to allow the smartly dressed woman to pass through on her way to piss through her tight fucking ass.

*

Along the corridors were paintings of families and guns, of dogs as bug-eyed as their one-time aristocratic owners and frantically gesticulating characters in scenes of religious life. She ran her hands along the striped wallpaper, into the noise of the main party. Up above on the ceiling, the painted circle of regretful gold faces, holding their precious manuscripts, raised saintly hands in admonishment and gazed anywhere but down at her.

As she passed one couple, they leant to whisper, their eyes on her face, then away when they saw that she had noticed. She felt emboldened and the 'wrong with' she'd apparently heard must mean Christopher.

Or that she was wrong. Good!

But all the same . . .

On the way to join the group around Angus, she asked the waiter hovering towards her with a tray of wine for a whisky. Evidently, the extreme nature of the request amused him enough.

'No – wait – my colleague here. This lady wishes for a whisky.'

'Certainly, madam. No please – we'll bring it to you . . .'

'In what way "wrong" I'd like to know . . .'

'Oh, don't go *on*!'

Laura had known that Angus was cross, and having joined his group again, had meant to angle her complaint into a humorous anecdote for all, but she had lost her touch, and recently all her words smeared into repetitious exaggeration of an evidently irritating nature.

One of his companions said to Angus, 'Oy, oy! What's up with you?'

'Well, this absurd upper-class world . . .'

'What world would you prefer?'

'The next.'

And the light from the chandelier shone on her face and she needed to sit. The chair gave her a view of the room, and there was a table beside it for her whisky glass. She felt a little sick, then closed her eyes, it passed.

From the table she picked up a hardback anthology of British poetry. Would Alison's dad be included? Probably not. She turned it over and saw the cover, and at once her heart was filled with exultation. She looked again. So. There was no doubt. Christopher was a petty, lecherous, fussing, evil old woman. He was a bully and a pedant. But he had once produced this. It was a depiction of two men grappling, but it made her breathless and have again the realities of bad times, like a time-lapse film of a rose flowering. Of the smell of damp and other chemicals in drug dealers' flats – and a more elusive little journey, a faltering little trail, bolstered now with the conviction (in spite of the world's hearty denials) – of emptiness. The dangers and the courage of these moments! And she felt grateful to him; the world was bigger for being so revealed.

Of course, it was not an endorsement for such times (that would have been indeed a suspiciously sentimental response) – no one could say that it glamorised them (why would they need that extra touch?).

It was dignity in reality. Some careful application of colour and now what imaginative dank pools are discovered in the far corner of the cave – not at all picturesque but teeming with unruly, indifferently ugly life.

She turned to see Angus beside her and held the book up to him casually, placing her hand over the title so only the painting was revealed.

After a moment she said, 'It does stand up.'

Angus nodded.

'It does stand up. Unlike his big dick.'

She laughed uproariously.

He added, enlivened by her laughter, 'Come on. We have a boy to meet.'

And they left the group who had begun laughing in expectation of further excesses to come, and who now had to move to warmer waters across the hall.

122

Chapter Twenty-two

'Were those the bath pearls that were his eyes?'

The party of four round at Martin's place had nudged and laughed each other into further silliness the evening before, making poems from the shower curtain patterns. Martin lay back in the tepid bath, smiling again as he looked at them now. 'Cotton wool' – a pot filled with child clouds, 'bath pearls' the same pot filled with grey balls stacked with pathetic abundance – his head was light with hangover. After they'd gone, he had slept fitfully and late and now he had to hurry. When he stepped down into West Richmond Street, he felt it more, shielding his eyes from the watered down afternoon sunlight and bending away from the sudden cold. Halfway down South Bridge, he saw the salutation across the street and raised his hand.

'Good *eve*ning!'

'You look rough – late night then, sir!'

'Oohh . . .'

The two of them laughed, bowed their heads in dignified sympathy. Last week it had emerged that they shared with him a distaste for the psychology professor's mode of sarcastic wit ('inadequacy, inadequacy!'). This confession had taken place in a drink after the last tutorial.

Martin could see that they were formulating some return to that subject, but wrapping his coat round himself and jogging in preparation for moving onwards, he shouted, 'Have to rush and meet someone off a train . . . Not the pace for a Saturday!'

'Not for any day!'

He waved his arm up behind him, but round the corner, he slowed down again. He had time enough, a brisk walk would get him there.

The shape of the distant mountains stirred some feverish ancestral pride, until he remembered the initial childish sightings of such and was overcome by more immediate and less exalted associations.

Laura's visit had been arranged in the first exultation of belonging. He had not experienced such easy camaraderie before. He had wished to show her off, and to her, his new status. But now, six months in, he didn't want the disturbance of other world visitations, the sort that would not settle unobtrusively into his gently established orbit. His parents had visited, but they had talked with soft voices and had responded to his companions' remarks with appreciative laughter. When they had left, nothing untoward remained, no evidence at all of their visit, except an imperceptible comet's tail of admiration, soon scattered into invisibility and forgotten.

He found them at the station barrier as planned. They had had to come from the other side of town. At Laura's suggestion, they went to the nearest pub for a drink, a place as dreary and damp as the Scottish weather outside.

Interrupting Angus's account of the book festival '. . . *so far* . . .' Laura asked them both with an attempt at discretion, 'Drink?'

'Coke, thanks'

'Proper drink?'

Martin involuntarily glanced at his watch, and Angus said, 'Oh, she's not bound by the tyrannies of time!'

But as Laura laughed rather too hilariously, on her way to the bar, Angus added, 'A few more decades behind that slap, several more pounds, do you not think she'll feel quite at home in this sort of establishment?'

Her wildly applied make-up and spindly looking legs had startled Martin, but Angus's animosity made him wary and resentful; he tried to be pleasant, to return to the subject of the book festival.

Had there been any questions?

'Yes – were any of the characters based on real people? (Of course! what do you think I do – make things *up*?)'

It was established that Angus wouldn't remain with them, the festival had paid for a night in the Holiday Inn ('or anyway, some such place – here . . . '). And Martin, squinting in the gloom, had been able to give directions from the almost illegible piece of paper handed to him.

'Another?'

'Haven't we had enough gaiety for one day?'

Outside, adjusting their eyes to the daylight, they waved him off and Martin and Laura walked along in silence. After a while, he started to ask questions about the family, and as he spoke, she could feel that he was avoiding glancing any more at her. Apparently he had been startled by her thinner appearance and she felt gratified.

He moved from polite concerns for Vivienne, to ask about Charles and Jeanette.

'They're now living in her house then?'

'Yes.'

'Nice house?'

'No.'

Infected by her boredom, he tried again with a yawn, 'Aarh, so it's love then?'

'Or convenience.'

He woke up for that – squinting up at the sunset behind the far hills. He thought of his elegant little romantic theories, as yet not fully tested.

'Surely that's rather a different thing?'

'Oh, all the bits and pieces fit together and it'll work all right.'

Passing the café, they saw the two friends that Martin had run into earlier. They made room for the two of them at their table in a hospitable way. They watched Laura with incredulity or dismay? – Martin couldn't tell – as, newly animated, she launched into her ribald tales. She gave casual accounts of the effects of amyl nitrite up old painters' noses (he saw their shrinking at the well-known name when it came) and of other friends whose exploits and names had a certain ring to them. But her listeners would have found it hard to recognise the emphasis as being a boastful one, since in their minds, friendship was not a subject that would need to fall into that elevated category.

Back at Martin's rented rooms, Laura lay on the single bed, underneath the flowered counterpane. She was reduced to a dry shell now that her audience was gone; everything had been used for their entertainment. Having sat with him in his sitting-room for some desultory chat, she had announced that she had to do some work on her own – she wasn't hungry. Now she could hear Martin pottering about next door – even these discreet little domestic clatterings had a ring of disapproval to them. She should get up, but her head went back to the centre again, her eyes on the ceiling. No, he was cross; his mannerisms had all the characteristics of sulkiness.

The Sunday lunchtime assembly was almost the same as the previous days, with the addition of one girl, who as the afternoon drew on, sat still in her chair, laughing quietly at the antics of the party. Laura could see which one of them was the joker of the group, but his teasing was confined to another – evidently it was an old theme, this one's Celtic gloom. Laura smiled too, although she was beginning to find the subject boring. At one point she threw in a subtle little comment on their imminent Highland trip, and though an outsider it seemed to have hit the mark. All the company laughed and looked at her anew.

It was always the same; Laura would make an effort to begin with. But at some point, just as Martin was beginning to feel – not quite proud and not quite happy – there would appear a little spasmodic jerkiness to her movements; had he imagined it? No. As she rose to pour herself another glass, her voice jumped in with disproportionate vigour. And her ignoring of the red wine spilt (why the hell hadn't he removed the lace cover?) was marginally less irritating than her frenzied efforts to help him dab it away once she turned and saw what she had done.

'Oh dear! Oh dear! And the nice white doily? No, tablecloth – ruined!'

'It's fine I'm sure.'

'But it will never be the same again – never as pure as when it emerged from its creator's crochet needles!'

'It's OK – I've added salt.'

But she had already lurched up and was on her way to his little kitchenette – it was hardly that comical – his landlady's taste! They had been through that subject once already, it was tiresome that it should be returned to repeatedly. He found it hard to control his tightening mouth, the joke, in its pointless trajectories, would doubtless end up on him.

'His work may be successful, but it is ugly for the sake of it.'

As Martin's friend announced this verdict, he picked up the photographs for another look and smiled; oh, she knew that sort of smile well – the smile of kindness present in certainty.

'After all, the art world imposes value on their designated works for economic reasons of its own. It has nothing to do with artistry or technique.'

'Actually, he is an excellent painter.'

She wasn't in love with Christopher, but she was true to herself when she argued that his work was of the highest level. However much he irritated her now with his pitiful attempts on the dance floor, reflected old and grey in the disco mirror, she wasn't going to descend into the belief that his work was only good in order only to bolster her esteem.

He placed the last of the photographs back on the coffee table, with a polite, 'Anyway, it's all subjective I suppose.'

'No, it's not.'

But he had tried to be tactful, and her furies were soothed by the attempt, if not the reasoning.

Angus's arrival with all the energy of disgust was a relief to all – the lumpen street crowds had not contained a single attractive face – what was it with his fellow Scots and their facial structure?

Laura watched Angus being monopolised, his novel praised. Laura understood that it was its rarity value that appealed to students of this sort, who mistrusted popularity. She watched sourly, despising their inability to disguise their enthusiasm. Oh yes – all superciliousness gone, *not* to be replaced by charm. One of them casually alluded to Otis Redding and Angus was able to correct him – the title was from a Bessie *Smith* song. 'Not there . . . ?' He broke into a little refrain – 'Once I lived the life of a millionaire . . .' Keeping an eye on their expectant faces, Angus continued more heartily with haughty disregard for rhythm, singing '. . . Taking all my friends out for a good time, drinking high class liquor, champagne and wine . . .'

With this distraction, Laura was able to pick up the photograph of her unfinished portrait and take it to her room. She thought of the reactions to it. Angus had handed it back to her at King's Cross station without comment, his eyebrows raised. She had a line of coke and looked at it again. It seemed quite good to her so far. Good enough? Perhaps too good. There was something about the juxtaposition of the toy and her prominently veined hand that seemed a little facile. Nothing was out of place, everything had a design. Perhaps that's what they meant.

She lay back on the bed. She felt somewhat dismal. She would have to dismiss from her head the childish notion that her talents lay in being an artist's muse. But it was worse than that. Her attachment had come after the glory was gone.

And if God wants our attention, what does he do? Gives us a sunset spreading its pastel prettiness over the greying hills and pleasing everyone. Big deal.

Having reached the top of the hill, they stood looking down on the lights of the town. The purple clouds streaked across the remains of the visible sky and the coconut smell from the yellow gorse bushes puffed towards them ('just a little suburban now that you mention it . . . ').

The stark northern hills were soon obliterated by the spreading darkness, leaving only the detail of the immediate surroundings. And suddenly it was the time of apathy when nature dropped its efforts, and backstage, so to speak, everything sat or hopped or waved desultorily, carrying out their functions with no meaning attached.

Martin asked Laura, 'Does this still make you think of God?'

Laura shifted impatiently.

'Is this the best He can do – the picturesque?'

('At least it *is* picturesque.')

And they all laughed. Laura saw that they had minded her artistic boastings. Listening to their sniggers, she felt some sympathetic bond with nature's indifference.

'Shall we go then?'

'Yes. Let's go and get a drink.'

'The pubs are closed Sunday afternoon.'

'Christ – we really are in the land of the puritans!'

Angus clapped his hands disgustedly as they stood, then continued, 'OK. Come on. It's my hotel bar then – and then on to the lowly clubs of Edinburgh!'

'Oh no – it's an early night for us, no *really* . . .'

They were more or less the only patrons of the spruce room. The barman saw nothing incongruous in the piped ballads, and took their orders for sandwiches and drinks with cosmopolitan disinterest.

On the way back from the lavatory, Laura pulled a leaflet out of the tourism box by the entrance. It featured a distant view of the Kentigern Abbey outline and an inset of the sea.

'Yes, very nice.'

Angus handed the leaflet back to her.

Her eyelids were held unnaturally wide in an effort to stop them closing. She said, 'How about going there. It's only an hour's drive away. For a picnic?'

'I don't think so. Ruins always rather depress me – old crumpled stones, old piles of Sunday newspapers somehow.'

And that was fair enough.

'Can't you *women* think of a thing to do?'

But the drugs that had led to this bout of erotic haziness had begun to wear off, leaving a rim of scum in Laura's stomach and head. She rose giddily from her unappealing task, glad that the lights of the town only partially lit the striped hotel room through the thin green curtains. Angus's grey stomach and large limp dick faded suitably into the gloom. It was nearly goddamned dawn. She pushed herself out of the bed, held out her hands blindly, padded tentatively into the bathroom.

Chapter Twenty-three

The walls were no longer striped because it was night. Laura's thoughts tortured themselves over the imperceptible distance and diminished. She had seen a film once, soldiers lying in a grey hospital ward, with nurses reluctantly tending. But here, the light drew stronger as if a theatre curtain had been pulled back on a cardboard stage. And as more was revealed, the blues and greens, too practical to be anything other than reality, the movie remained like a film over her vision. She closed her eyes; she was back with the immobile survivors in that grey romantic vision of purgatory.

But yes, she could talk, and so she tried to sleep again. But then she hurtled towards the same face, expressionless and dull like a statue with all the art sucked away and it was her face.

She opened her eyes again. She was in the correct place for death, every modern convenience and no apologies needed. Her heart slowed a fraction. She was dismayed to find herself telling the man by her side about the moment on the beach, a block in her head that needed rearranging. He nodded, pulling at one side of the bed, then moving round to the other.

'You know I'm a nurse not a psychiatrist, don't you?'

'No.'

'That means I can't prescribe you any medication.'

'Right.'

'I expect Dr Wallace will be along . . .'

She woke to find that she couldn't remember what he'd said – but it had been a dream surely? Who cares.

She was in a room alone. But beside her was her father. He seemed restrained, but his hands were crawling all over each other.

'Did you hear that?'

'Yes.'

'I'm fine now.'

'Good.'

His voice was kind.

'I need someone, I'm going to be sick.'

Her father's face dissolved into fragments and she closed her eyes.

Charles and Vivienne listened as it was explained that there would be unlikely to be any permanent damage. She could be kept in the hospital for a week so that her progress could be monitored and then she could move to outpatients.

'I gather she was brought here by a friend?'

'Yes. Lucky.'

Charles didn't like to examine the odds further. Instead, he turned efficient, giving an account of Angus's brisk thinking, getting her straight to the hospital, having had to carry her to the empty reception of the hotel in which they had been staying.

'Yes, I met him. The writer.'

'Yes.'

'With whom I believe she is writing something?'

'I don't know anything about that.'

After a while, the doctor looked back at his notes.

'Now. I should ask you if she has ever exhibited any symptoms of eating disorders?'

'Not that I know of.'

'Well. Her liver count is high, indicating a high degree of alcohol consumption but I don't think she can have been taking heroin for too many years since she has only moderate symptoms of physical addiction. But what with her level of incoherence and distress, I think that we may have to face the possibility that this overdose was a deliberate cry for help.'

The doctor faced them again grimly, behind his authority a hint of bewilderment severely curtailed. But surely he had seen similar cases before?

'I don't know why they do it.'

He pulled himself together. He explained he was a medical doctor who also had training in psychotherapy. He had an office in London, he was shortly to move back down there again, but he explained too, that he would like to keep her there, in the Paddington wing for the time being.

'Will she be receiving medication – of any sort?'

He looked down at his desk, frowning.

'Oh, normally in drug-related cases, we would be avoiding sedatives wherever possible. But since she is in considerable distress . . .'

Vivienne interrupted, asked if she should cancel her trip.

He looked up surprised. 'Oh I don't think that's necessary, as long as one of you is here. She'll be back in London by the time of your return.'

Charles explained that he would be staying nearby for the short term.

'Good, more convenient than to travel all this way for such short visits.'

'Oh I'm used to weekend trips up the A1.'

Dr Wallace's face turned suddenly genial in response to Charles's wry turn of phrase – oh he did appreciate charm!

So it seemed, that on these scales, as the pan containing the pills lightened, the other containing the future went down, weighed heavy with responsibility. But as her tears continued to come (much to her consternation and dislike) a few extra pills were supplied and up it went again with a clang, desirously light and airy. Whoever can witness this delicate balance in a family illness without wondering if some well meaning but oafish prod of help wouldn't weigh the mechanism down permanently on one side?

In the first rush of confusion, the hospital authorities had asked Charles to consider the question of keeping her in for a length of time, should they and he have felt it necessary for her own wellbeing. But this looked unlikely now – instead they talked of lessening the medication, and of Laura's return to London in the near future.

Was Charles relieved? To have to sit back and witness the awful delicate intricacy being reintroduced, the gossamer wires that miraculously should work together to produce balance. Charles was from the real world, this psychiatric wing held no attractions for him, but how could he help the wish that the decelerating tick tock of the mechanism might be weighted down safely with the reassuring imbalance of heavily prescribed drugs? Those drugs that would prevent once and for all, any pretence that the trepidatious, nail-biting high-wire act of balance be set once more in motion for all to have to watch.

For some time now, Laura had been a gathering weight and a responsibility for which he had absolutely no solution. The few times he had seen her recently, she had seemed wild-eyed and vague. Her eyes darting around, talking of grand schemes ahead and accepting all too quickly the after-dinner liqueur and then another. After the last dinner in his new house, Jeanette had said: 'She's just finding it hard to accept me.' And the awkwardness of that partial truth had forced Charles to change the subject and override his foreboding.

During her childhood, he had been able to leave the running of her life to those who knew better. Occasionally he enjoyed being the recipient of her affection. One morning, shortly before the move, she had visited him in the library and had handed him her offering. The little drawing, now hung in the bathroom of his new home, had been of them both at the river. It was quite clear that her arms were meant to be holding the fishing line for him, the dog was sitting too. The trees on the other side of the river had a profusion of painstaking leaves, and so there were only three of them, four with the blue-coloured onlooker across the river. The abbey was yellow like a house.

But over it now, rose the nave in deft lines. Coming in the

morning of Laura's presentation of the gift, Vivienne had demonstrated the necessity of its inclusion – accuracy! She had put down her pencil and examined the result, had listened with satisfaction to Laura's compliments.

Chapter Twenty-four

With Christopher Kovel's late night call fresh in his mind, full of obscure information (her psychological archetype and so on) – and flattering anxiety, Dr Wallace visited Laura two days running, sat by her bed. His brother was a sculptor and he felt to be himself moulded from a similar school of individualists. He thought he could discover a clue that would elude a less religious seeker. Both he and Laura longed to please each other but she could think of nothing to say. He asked if in her childhood there had been any traumas? The large woman in the next bed rose and shuffled briskly towards the door, turning back with the ubiquitous 'I'm off. All right, duck?' delivered with the characteristic vagary that rendered the inhabitants' self-absorbed company as soothing as solitude.

'There was one thing.'

And Laura was able to come up with the incident on the beach. As the basic facts emerged, Dr Wallace twisted forward with sympathy, but struggled to contain himself.

'Oh, it's not surprising, it's not surprising.'

But his conclusion was surprising. He seemed (and could she believe her luck?) to be justifying her drug-taking. And so there, to her relief, was the answer. She had felt bad at the time but felt worse now, dragging this shapeless spectre back, her hand in his, to shoulder the blame for her aimless path that had led to this, her violent black despair.

'But you know drugs don't help?'

'Yes. Yes, I do.'

She nodded her head, her mind agog with planning, fighting through the underwater weight of medication.

'It's a terrible trauma to have lived through, and not to have told anyone . . .'

She examined this possibility, but made no comment.

His face was – quizzical? She searched for the word, as his sympathy retreated like the rush of the tide, whose return might carry conditions.

'That's all I can remember I'm afraid.'

'Yes, well I think you're doing well. You'll be out of here soon.'

And his mouth opened and shut, suggesting and advising in a most discreet manner the way forward during those days ahead. She had to be excused.

Pushing through each institutional swing door, each one closer to the final one, the one through which it would be possible to fall into the olive-green-painted fields, and gaze at the fluorescent blue skies with the enviable ease of timelessness.

Dr Wallace opened the door to his office himself, with a significant look of regret. He was younger than Charles but his manner was weighty with sorrow. He pulled up a chair for Charles and then sat himself, for a moment silent.

'I think we have our reason.'

He did not allow his eyes to flinch from Charles's growing anguish, as he told the story in plain language. Then he remained with his hands folded, allowing Charles to assimilate this awful tale.

'And apparently she didn't tell anyone?'

Charles felt sick and impotent with fury over a decade too late. He had to clear his throat.

'Not that I know.'

'This sort of trauma can absolutely be the cause of this sort of incident – but with more talking, I think we can expect a profound change.'

Having left the office, Charles found it necessary to sit down in the plastic corridor chair. For once he was impervious to the smells and underhand noises from shuffling patients, always in the background. Having created a life of dullness for himself, now remorse was back, enlivening him horribly. He couldn't help the feeling that had he still been married to Vivienne, he would now be participating in her shrill analysis, burning off its worst excesses with an anaesthetising self-pity.

Chapter Twenty-five

Had she mentioned damp? Laura felt damp and that was unfortunate. Something about secretions was a revelation too far sitting in Dr Wallace's dry convenient office. His sympathy was for dry words, exact building blocks of clear message. And her damp hands reaching out with 'I love you' towards –

They met every afternoon in his office alone, evidence of her growing strength. Dr Wallace apparently relished the horrors that had been inflicted on her, since he encouraged more and more detail. It had become the routine subject to return to.

'How old was he?'

'I don't know.'

By this point, she hardly knew if he had existed at all and she didn't care to analyse this hazy dimness. She looked around at Dr Wallace's abysmal tribal artefacts, creation emerging from the mouths of coupling creatures. He looked at her pasty face and wondered.

He asked, 'You think this new medication is having the desired effect?'

'Yes.'

She hardly slept with it, but lay immobile, her thoughts racing. When she did sleep, her dreams were crammed with exhausting detail.

'Do you dream?'

'Yes.'

'Can you remember any of them now?'

'No.'

She preferred thinking to talking and at night she lay awake thinking and writing notes. If restless, she would join the blank night nurse in the smoking area, the classics professor too, sitting alone, the puff of stale chemicals off his blue dressing-gown the occasional reminder of his condition. From time to time he walked to the window, rigid with distaste. The stars and their sticky sleight of hand – stretching nebulous dreams out of empty vessels! He would never allow the hospital to dictate to him its own tyrannous superficiality, having constructed from his considerable knowledge a flimsy framework for ideas about his own lifestyle.

'Now.'

Dr Wallace tapped his teeth with his pen, perhaps suspecting her reservations. She looked up and he placed his pen on the desk, then his palms, flat.

'I'm going to suggest something.'

'Yes?'

'I'm going to suggest that over the next few days, you write down what you can about the incident and see what comes . . .'

He went to the back of his office, found in a drawer some large pieces of foolscap and another pen, and put these implements down in front of her.

After a moment he prompted her with, 'What do you think?'

She couldn't stand his nerves!

'Fine.'

'OK.'

And then he showed her out, holding the door open with a regretful look of encouragement.

That night she couldn't sleep and went again to the smoking area. There the professor was standing by the window. He spoke to himself precisely and at length of Odysseus's foe Charybdis, apparently looking at the grotesquely exposed roots of the tree in the yard, frothing and reaching up from their rightful place underground. With all his esoteric allusions, it crossed Laura's mind that he might have read *Desecration of My Kingdom*, King Freddie's book, or know of it, but he was not one for inviting enquiry.

Extinguishing her cigarette in the sand of the ashtray, she went back and, perching on her bed, wrote a piece then, talking of monstrous visions in solitary rooms, of other mirages smashed and of the truthful element that did still haunt her. After she had struggled away from the water to which he was pulling her, he had held her down in a businesslike grip, and she had leant up to kiss him, to say 'I love you' in an attempt at charm. But the pressure of the strangling scarf had prevented sound.

At their next session, if Dr Wallace was delighted with the brief scan of the written work, he was professional enough to disguise it.

'I'm going to look at this properly later. But did you feel you got anywhere?'

'Sort of.'

'Well done.'

He ushered her towards the door, his abstracted form especially pronounced. He held out his hand.

'Next week then.'

Alone in his office, he looked again at the paper and at once abstract delights burst forth in his mind, giving rise to intense contentment. Its obtuse symbolism delighted him.

The following week, he alluded to the session to Christopher with whimsical choice of dissimulation. Christopher was extremely concerned with his health and had a superstitious fondness for effective doctors. Three years previously Dr Wallace had found himself next to Christopher at a dinner. He had not been fazed by his unlikely neighbour, had talked on blithely and Christopher had responded. Sometime after this, Christopher had rung him for advice on who to turn to for a persistent cramp in his arm that was hindering work. After some diligent research through his files, Dr Wallace had recommended he contact an alternative practitioner, who had indeed cured the complaint with a mixture of homeopathy and manipulation. Ever since that time, Christopher rang

Dr Wallace from time to time and met him for dinner. He found his dry manner amusing, and since his artistic views were so wide of the mark, he indulged them. Dr Wallace in his turn was amused by Christopher's serene formality.

At first Christopher had been shocked to the point of frozen ineptitude by the news from Scotland, but he had recovered from this initial consternation more swiftly than the depth of his infatuation might have suggested. He had the old-fashioned view that this accident would have shocked Laura into dislike of the drug once and for all, since he could hardly conceive of the delicate enjoyments of the narcotic's effects being continued through the tidal wave inconvenience of addiction.

'So you think she might be better now.'

'Oh yes, oh yes.'

Dr Wallace cut and ate his food with gloomy precision.

'A terrible incident.'

While waiting for the main course, he livened up, started describing the exploration in some detail. '. . . My idea merely was that out of trauma should emerge a creative energy of some sort –'

But Christopher manoeuvred the conversation away by means of dextrous silence; his fondness didn't extend infinitely.

Chapter Twenty-six

Angus stirred from his bar stool, then remained there.

The owner asked, 'Another?'

'In a minute. Just waiting for someone.'

It was five in the afternoon. The owner refused to give in to premature gloom, asking archly, 'Oh?'

Angus didn't answer. At that moment, Catherine arrived through the door, her vivacity not matched by the trailing Tom, who as ever, radiated a lack of curiosity as if it were a virtue.

At once, in her brisk way, Catherine asked matter-of-fact questions as to what exactly had happened up there. Tom assumed a conventional concern for Laura's predicament. It was true that now she had hit such an unlikely low, he felt more interested in her. As Angus spoke, Catherine half listened and looked around appreciatively at the alien environment. The converted attic room at the top of many narrow stairs contained only a small bar and benches underneath the two windows. Outside Gerard Street's gay Chinese banners flapped with amusing infrequency.

Drink held before his face, Angus finished, '. . . I didn't realise *girls* were so heavy.'

Catherine turned her attention back to him with punctilious respect.

'Now. She would be dead if it wasn't for you!'

'Mm.'

'So what's all this about a wasted life?'

The club's owner, polishing glasses with a proprietorial flourish, had to concede that this was an amusing line. Normally he monopolised the conversation with his controversial views on capital punishment. But before he could join in, it became clear that it had almost come to the end, Catherine's short-lived enchantment with Angus's dreary attempts to enter the fun. Certainly her indulgence for the sloping ceilings and floors of this club had reached an end. The few boys sitting with drab apathy hardly inspired gaiety! Because there were so few of them she felt they must be automatically a part of their group. She looked at her watch, jumped up and clapped her hands.

'Right. It's time to go! Whoever wants to join us to meet a friend who is back in London after having been – ill – is welcome!'

But there were no stirrings at this amicable proposition. The boys had their own agenda and this offer was not enough to deflect them from their passive task. They remained, sitting on the wooden seats, waiting to catch whomsoever would emerge and reward their vigil.

And Angus too declined the invitation. He had no wish to see Laura. The incident had not added to his life. It had enfeebled him and he resented her.

Chapter Twenty-seven

Occasionally Laura woke to find that great tracts of time had been effectively obliterated. It scarcely bore examination – this peculiar void. It was gone, so not worth bothering about. That was the point of inebriation after all.

But something prevented her ringing some of the party from the night before and revealing her ignorance again. As careless toward convention though they were, increasingly nowadays their looks towards her contained suggestions of disapproval, as if discussions had taken place behind her back. She had been back for a month, but added to her natural ineptitude was now the further embarrassment of the official stamp of inadequacy.

Today she could place only the moment when they had gone back to a flat – whose? She examined the images in her memory, and realised it was this one, hers.

Every morning consciousness shocked her a little. And through closed eyelids the twinkling shards of sunlight prickling her skin prevented a return to sleep. But she could go and get another bottle of whisky – that ineffective bypass to an anyway unsatisfactory destination.

Passing the Arabic idlers, the Odeon's gargantuan advertisements, the local aspects that usually pleased her, she found herself flooded with chemicals of panic that having finished with the brain, diverted their excess to her neck and heart. She made herself sit on a bench in the park, her heart squeezing out its rapid beats with fractious and painful irregularity. She thought of her heart – imagined its shape from books. There it was, like a familiar celebrity, looking just like it ought. She willed it to calm down. But sweat poured out of her face, cold. She longed for the concealment of habit but every cell was forming and replacing itself, alive on the park bench, the possibility of reformulation a hideous reality. She had no wish to die, or worse, be taken ill, here out in the open.

Christopher had liked tales from the hospital, especially those concerning the professor, but increasingly he shifted around as she sat in his kitchen, idly reading the tabloids. It was easier to be away from him and he didn't put up any objections.

Now one dog was over-enthusiastic and was wearing a cheap collar that made Laura feel sorry for it. It had grabbed another dog's toy and was running in large circles at top speed, its eyes shining with excitement, not knowing that the spectators did not share its amusement. Was it the cheap material collar that made them despise it?

She felt the alcohol tremendously surging, attempting every route to bring the same optimism as its first appearance in the bloodstream. But she knew it would always be an unsatisfactory chemical; there were better out there, put on this earth to numb and calm.

It was hardly as though the doughy dreamlike natives of her previous environment could be preferred, but she missed them, absurdly. The daily group sessions had been restful and regular; she could remain silent in the face of interminable complaint, minutely dealt with by the nurses with weary diligence as if embarking on an allegorical quest. At night, these same preoccupations, confined as they were within individual radiuses, left her just as alone and cosseted. During those nights, she had felt warm with contentment at having pledged to herself that her heroin days were over. No additions had been needed in that safe two-dimensional land. But, of course, now she was back in the real world of accident and extreme, where every failure produced punishing chemicals, and effort to push past obstacles, be pushed in turn – she knew that by evening she would be whirling in all directions with the tidal forces, longing for closure.

She made an instinctive decision, and immediately these atoms and corpuscles returned to a coherent and dazzling beat, shimmering in correct patterns like summer flies. The familiar buildings, dull signposts indicating she was moving in the right direction, now were doors that would open up to significant and rich and satisfying new worlds. The jewels would be somewhere nearby, pouring up all around.

Banks always caused her unease, but the cash was handed over with not so much as a look. At a telephone box, she made a call. She was expecting that this would have to be the first of many calls, many trails, but instead, she was told it was OK, but that she'd have to wait. At once, her expectation was undermined by impatience. She had been alive for a second, but now, having her goal in sight, she felt bored at the prospect of the time she had to kill. Finally it was there. She arrived at the correct door at the correct time, and was let in. Once up the narrow stairs, she sat in the orange chair, listening to the grievances of her dealer, not liking to add to them with a request for a smoke. Finally some tin foil was offered her way, and she took it with polite restraint, a little disappointment crept over the expected satisfaction of closure. Was it only for this that she was losing her soul? Yeah, well, why the fuck not.

When she returned to her flat, there was a message. It was from Tom, casually suggesting she give him a call? She was able to do so without any hint of nerves since for the time being, she no longer had any.

Chapter Twenty-eight

As he listened to his son talking of his new night-club venture, Edward nodded and smiled and looked at Laura's pale face, her eyes half closed, as she too joined in with a semblance of appreciation. Edward remembered her as a child, but he was not sentimental, contrary to popular belief. Though good-natured, he had only the family feelings that were absolutely necessary. His son he admired and supported, but it was plain to all that he was absolutely uninterested in him on any profound level. This freedom suited Tom; he was as super-cilious as his father was benign.

'Coming to my opening night then?'

'Of course! I'll be there!'

Laura stirred herself.

'Great!'

Edward liked her enthusiasm and as always he admired her looks that were of such old-fashioned construction. He could see that his son was not by any means smitten, and in the interests of truth admitted to himself that Laura was somewhat his superior. Tom was clever enough, but not original, and that was perhaps his good fortune. All his efforts went towards his rather successful financial ventures, and (Edward gave a mental sigh of weariness) a very good thing too.

He asked about her father, and rather than reveal any piti-ful and dull details of his present life, Laura told him the story of the toad, the one that she and Martin had pestered Charles for on every car journey. Edward liked the tale; she had known he would.

He rose and then turning from the pile of records in the corner of the room, said, 'I'll play you a song. "King Kong Kitchie kitchie Ki-mi-o".'

She laughed and he did too as it came on, whistling badly and waving his fingers to the little beat.

Tom assumed a dismissive tone, 'Oh – Froggie goes a courting.'

But he laughed too; he had inherited his father's taste in obscure musical gems.

The next day Christopher took her roughly to one side.

'Can't you see he's a cunt?'

'I thought you liked the look of his face?'

'But it has disintegrated into the sort of mediocrity that will take over once the novelty of youth has worn off.'

But they had a painting to finish and Christopher was full of anguish.

Recently he'd had meetings with the curator of a large gallery in which they had talked of a huge exhibition of old and new works. It would take at least eighteen months to organise, but it was clear that a corner had been turned. Christopher had always had admirers, his work had always been taken seriously. But this would move everything to a whole new echelon.

But as to whether this would penetrate his splendidly arrogant isolation and affect his judgement – not at all. He quite overturned the accepted view that creators work best from a position of weakness, that their works are products of the terror of failure emerging bit by bit from feeble fingers. He carried on with the same stern standards. He had never allowed visions of how success might affect his work and he had always had the sort of sexual success that can intoxicate the newly celebrated.

But now he was dreary with distaste and jealousy. Waking that same afternoon, to find him gone from the room, Laura rose and came upon him lying on the bathroom floor, mute. She was surprised by her lack of involvement. If any feelings of justification stirred, they were those of a vandal faced with their handiwork across a national treasure.

149

'Sorry, I'll just get . . .'

She stepped delicately over his body in order to reach her jacket, took it and stepped back, closing the door behind her on her way back to her position on the bed.

From its opening night, Tom's basement club 'Sparks' made a lively feature of playing old obscure songs alongside the contemporary ones and soon it began to have small lines of people queuing outside, waiting for its opening time, eleven o'clock. Even a year ago, Laura knew that the humorous and charming aspects of this sort of club would have got her dancing wildly to the old songs on the packed dance floor and collapsing to sing its praises to the already converted standing drinking at the bar. Now, she realised that those irregular days of extreme emotional energy were gone, she was in the heavy consistent hands of the drug that removed these wayward and embarrassing high spirits, and the drunken despair too that had regularly hit her at the end of those nights.

She recovered some money selling little bags made up from the large amount she was now buying for herself. Having acquired the reputation of having enough to sell, soon there were gathering numbers circling round her and requesting their share. Reluctant though she was to let go of any of her stash, these grudging transactions meant that she almost had enough to buy the next amount without having to resort to borrowing money off Tom – an unpleasant task that involved the use of acting. He mistrusted all but the most insouciant arrogance, and since she never repaid him, her efforts had to be more extreme each time.

Never having experienced life with a junkie before, he had never encountered selfishness that eclipsed his own and he found he had a certain fascination for this lawless and limitless trait. She had assured him that she and Christopher were just on professional terms now and pride had prevented his usual indifference – he wasn't frightened! Laura had almost smiled at his manner, but she found that the process involved was mechanical. She assumed that Tom's humourless state came from having been surrounded by its most insistent manifestations most of his life, but having found the means to smother these sparks and dissatisfactions in herself, Laura too found this deadened state restful.

During the times of withdrawal when humour and sexual desire heaved their way back in again, she found herself longing to shut their high spirits the fuck up. Unable to rest, she would lie in bed, reading, cramming in marmalade smeared on bread, but the strings of saliva stretched from the dry bread to her mouth, prevented progress. And all the time her reproductive organs rippled into grasping life.

She knew that each time she returned to the drug, she was being dragged further and further down, but when forced to emerge back into the light, she thought most urgently of her forfeited refuge. Self-conscious and gasping with involuntary laughter, damp and disorientated, each movement awkward and an effort in an alien environment, she would long to disappear back down into the dry darkness of the retreat, although the time would come when she would no longer return.

'Coming?'

She raised herself, but tonight on the way to the club, they had one of their usual arguments. Tom disliked losing his cool, but her wan disgust, squashed against the corner of the taxi, wiping her hands on her jeans, was unflattering. Once there, they divided off to attend to their individual tasks, his inside, checking the sound and the bar, Laura's to head to a flat in a nearby street. There, she had to wait, since she had committed the offence of not having rung first. By the time of her return, she expected further signs of affront, but the club was now open and she was able to slip past the dance floor towards the lavatory.

'. . . this song's for Laura – "Ain't Got No Home" by the great Frogman.'

151

But Laura was engrossed with her purchase in the dank cubicle. Though she heard Tom's announcement through the mic, then Clarence Frogman Henry's delightful melodic switches, her veins made no concessions to fucking romantic gestures.

Chapter Twenty-nine

To Christopher, Charles's face was grand. And being receptive to aristocratic monuments of unapologetic plainness, the sort that the ignorant might find unappealing, he was naturally convinced by it, liked it. Charles's blushing face now had a peculiar look of shy knowledge shared, his amused eyes flickering towards his guest's as if to apologise for levity. He was touching on some of his schemes, with which he hoped to make money. The details were small but piled together they were ambitious.

Christopher listened, his face by no means impassive, but his discomfort was unreadable to the increasingly enthusiastic Charles.

Christopher had no respect for consistency; in those he despised, indolence was a characteristic of the very weakness he loathed. But snobbishly, he liked observing idleness in those he admired, imagining that it added to the subtle charm radiating from the rarer circles they moved in. He liked Charles, and he would have preferred that he return to such a life of unemployment than participate in these fruitless schemes: tax breaks and undiscovered links and the profit to be had from strategic introduction.

Had Laura been there, he would have explained afterwards in some tortuous detail that since the venture was bound to fail, it seemed unbecoming to a man with natural dignity – even if he needed money. And *did* he? Such people, he would have claimed, had so little sense of financial reality – but Laura was not there.

Charles felt a little deflated that his modest boasts were making no headway. He had thought that Christopher, with his notorious love of the underworld, would have appreciated the suggestion of a scam.

And so they got on to the subject that was the reason for their meeting – Laura's arrest for heroin supply. She had been arrested following the discovery of heroin on one of her more indiscreet clients, who having tottered and sprawled embarrassingly in front of two police officers, dropping her little stash at their feet, was quick to shift the blame for her fall to another.

'Do you think it will affect the sentencing that she is now in this rehabilitation place?'

'Oh yes, I think so.'

'How long do they say she will need to be there?'

'Right up until the court case I believe.'

Christopher put down his coffee cup.

'But these sorts of drug institutions are so humourless – do you think their methods will actually do her good?'

Charles was put into a moral dilemma since this criticism was so aligned to his own suspicions. But as a father talking to his daughter's most unsuitable lover (even – the cause of her downfall it had been whispered by the unimaginative) his loyalty had to side with convention.

'I think so, all things considered . . .'

In the last few months it had crossed Charles's mind that Laura might die. He had not understood this in a theoretical way, but with the same absolute clarity of a telephone ringing. When the first telephone call had come from the assigned lawyer at the police station, full of cheery pessimism as he broke the news, moving to the subjects of probable bail conditions and likely outcomes, Charles had felt surprised by his own anger, since a worse message had been avoided. And then Christopher had rung and had offered information he had on good lawyers – he had spoken to friends . . . it had been a disconcerting telephone call but a welcome one. It relieved him from the humiliating admission that he could think of nothing constructive. Now Christopher started on the subject.

'The lawyer has helped a friend of mine – not a drug case, but a serious one, he is expensive but, I believe, good.'

Charles scribbled down the information as it came. He then put down the pen, and listened to Christopher as he started on the delicate subject of women's prisons. For one so consumed with the aesthetic pleasures of low life and considering also his attraction to the perverse, Christopher seemed to be taking a conventionally horrified line at the thought that Laura might find herself mixing in such company.

The next day, Vivienne was amused by the description of Christopher's concerns. She said, 'It proves we do all become more conservative with age.'

Charles and Vivienne were closer now than they had been when they were married. They had lunch on a regular basis and these meetings were kept from Jeanette by Charles. Had either of them had the necessary ingredients to their characters, these occasions might have been romantic, since there was more than a little yearning in the air. But Vivienne was too insistent on the shortcomings in her life and Charles had stubbornly determined on his contentment; the two pictures could not have blended into one, the pieces even jammed together wouldn't have fitted.

And the less Charles had need to worry about Vivienne, the more he did so, because he was lonely. Since the divorce, she was in fact happy. She travelled a great deal and would have found that she enjoyed single life but for her certainty that it was in some way deficient.

Charles looked round at the new acquisitions. He recognised and admired impeccable taste and had always resisted the lure of his inherited desire for the utilitarian, his parent's preferred choice. Vivienne's insistence on genuine style had somewhat oppressed him too, but now sitting in the elegant room of her new flat, he glanced about with something like dreariness – it was perfect. Was it original? No, correct.

Vivienne returned with the coffee. She raised the bottle and her eyebrows in a question and he replied in his rather diffi-dent way, charming because quite aware of the little irony, 'I think I *will* have a little!'

She added a little brandy to the coffee, saying, 'I think this occasion calls for a little help.'

Neither wanted to disrupt the pleasant atmosphere by beginning on the subject.

'Well . . .'

But familiarity had not dulled the unexpected pleasure he got from looking at her. It was a pleasure and an effort to be in her company, he couldn't ignore the poignancy that the glamour of her good looks provided. And all the time he nodded and laughed in agreement with whatever tale she was telling only so as to be able to look and look and analyse. Finally he had to come in with his own talk.

'I'm going down to visit Laura at the weekend with Jeanette.'

'Oh good. I'm away – and' – could she interpret his intent look correctly? – 'I'm not sure I could *quite* face another fami-ly therapy session so soon . . . I'll go for the weekend visit after this one.'

Vivienne still had the obscure sense that she would be held to account for her daughter's fall – though Laura's assigned counsellor had made every effort to establish that the guilt lay only with Laura herself.

Going through the front door of the treatment centre, Charles kept Jeanette ahead of him, his hand on her back in a push disguised to seem companionable. Each step shuffled him delicately from pompous indifference back to shy antago-nism. The middle-aged administrator who appeared in the hall walked jauntily but could not suppress her dominance as she surveyed the arrivals, some of whom were patients, some relatives. She held her hands above her head, clapped them humorously together once.

'In this room if you're coming to group!'

Her eyes passed over Charles and Jeanette; her smile of acknowledgement was as cursory as their appearance was ordinary. Her supreme leadership skills did not extend to concealment of boredom, nor her spiritual beliefs to egalitarianism.

Charles had not the means of raising himself and chuckled ingratiatingly.

'Oh, yes. Thank you.'

Already seated, Laura saw the conventionally dressed couple enter the room and acknowledged their grimacing smirk of greeting with a raised hand. They walked heavily, he jumped away to allow a bolder woman access to his armchair, laughed politely in her direction, but this was overlooked. He and Jeanette found themselves places, she had to bring another chair into the circle so as to sit next to him, but everyone shuffled round amiably.

The administrator started the meeting and were there any unlikely timid disclosures from family members present, they were scorched back by her severe smile and brisk manner. She spoke of sentimental inaccuracies allied to the disease of addiction (nodding to her familial audience with an assumption of their acquiescence). She outlined the simple yet necessarily arduous stages of recovery – acknowledgement, shedding of guilt, and finally, the salvation of a truthful life. Her listeners were astounded into silence.

She moved without flourish to talk of recurrent manifestations of disease, pausing between each to look around with effective emphasis. She spoke of seemingly steady households being disrupted by a member's alcoholism or addiction. Of solid structures being eroded with unseemly rapidity through exposure to the gambling addict's habitual symptoms.

Although he froze uncomfortably, no one looked towards Charles, or even thought to include him in this last assessment.

He had assumed the bourgeois lifestyle entirely and now nothing was left of the grandeur Laura had initially alluded to as having been lost. Having seen them enter the room, even

Laura herself could hardly believe in the one-time existence of royal connections and once-acclaimed estates. The tales of past splendour could only be thought of as being as inconsequential as a ladybird accidentally alighting on an expensive leaf – picturesque until blown off again.

The alcoholic newcomer was a sly one. For the first few days he did nothing more than sit with apparent obedience in group, nodding at whatever was said. Only the occasional subversive laugh at nothing much indicated his lack of commitment. He was quite prepared to accept the authority of Laura's month-long residency, they knew each other already very slightly. But most evenings she was unable to prevent trivia winning out over duty at least for some of the time. She could see that the others in the room thought these reminiscences indulgent. But tonight, emboldened by their shared tales of Edward Kielder's more preposterous theories, high spirits had lit her up; she told the story of the legend of Kentigern Abbey, ostensibly to him, but to the room at large, trying to align it with the spirituality they spoke of here. There had been a few nods, a slight air of disapproval.

As she climbed the stairs, she knew that she had probably only just escaped the always hovering accusation of 'grandiosity'. But, anyway, who would believe that even such gravity as existed in this little tale could ever have extended to the man who had arrived the weekend before with such lack of fanfare? Certainly none of a saint's violent modesty had been visible (thank the Lord in one way). Instead, the unassuming ordinariness of an unexamined life had settled heavily on her father's quilted shoulders and sluggish features.

Upstairs, she took advantage of the rare solitude in the room and lay on the bed. She thought some more of her father and that she too would have to look for a similarly placid lifestyle without any sort of glamour or acclaim within it. That was realism. Christopher was snobbish, but, after all, he was an artist. Snobbery rushing back to its furthest limit –

speed transforms into time and disappears. And now out of this timeless, motionless swamp, clambers out with no grace, the ungainly and disgusting, unhygienic impulse towards art, sainthood, destruction or boredom. And much as they talked about God here, and humility, they had no thought of the saint's patient little journey alone and smelling foully, alight with hideous fervency, milling ecstatically amongst the animals.

Christopher was not a saint but a genius – but still – one of God's chosen. And if God were going to choose, he might as well pick the gratifying ones. If not the saints who glow with devotion and doubt, then the artists who radiate with the fury of having been picked and who use every aspect of their dragged up gifts to sneer at their disgusting patron.

But the counsellors here made it their business to prise any suggestion of passion from infantile hands, replacing it with the easy discipline of ordinary life; religious ecstasy was an indulgence, amorous ecstasy a myth, the mysteries deftly removed and concealed. And what was wrong with that? Nothing at all. The path of life being laid out before her in practical terms, had for Laura, the intriguing nature of novelty. She felt peaceful, and the missing ingredients were unlamented.

Chapter Thirty

They all sat together in the court number three waiting room. Charles and Vivienne felt it correct that they desist from small talk. Instead they stared ahead at the blue walls, suitably and silently distressed. After a while, Jeanette followed their example, though it sat uneasily since she had the extra tingling nerves of Vivienne's presence to cope with. It was hardly the time to seem nervily mute! But Dr Wallace had his professional pride and so asked Laura bland questions at an irregular rate.

'You've been in rehabilitation for – how long?'

'Two months.'

'And you feel it has been beneficial?'

'Yes – very.'

'Why is that?'

As she answered, Laura felt the resentful clouds of compromise rushing to fill her determinedly bland skies. She knew he would have no interest in the prosaic formula of the treatment programme since it defied his belief in the lifesaving jewels of inconsistency. Evidently he did feel himself let down by her lapse, since his eyes grew vague.

'Well. That perhaps will affect the sentencing.'

They all sat silently and listened to the distant noise of screams and doors slamming. He ignored their unspoken assumption that he should investigate and returned to the previous subject.

'That's outside my field. You understand the difference don't you?'

'Yes.'

He had with him an umbrella, and he slapped it lightly against his palm with a vaguely military rhythm. He clearly felt it made him look foolish and it did.

She asked, 'Have you ever met anyone you consider to be evil?'

Oh and then his face lit up! She had expected the cold dark prodding talk of background abuse and neurological damage. But why not allow a touch of the mystique of the old days? After all, everyone likes a tiny bit of colour in their lives – a little peak at the imaginative world of God.

He let slip the answer – 'I *have* . . .'

But having to restrain himself – he was there in a professional capacity after all! – he put down the umbrella absently, ready to give a careful answer. But at that moment an officer appeared and announced that it was time. He picked up his umbrella and with it a disagreeable distance settled over him again.

The procedure had been short, Laura's plea of guilty had seen to that. She had been placed in the holding cells, judging by the grumbling chat of the officers escorting her, to await a minicab to take them all to Holloway.

When she'd left that morning, everyone had gathered with sincere concern and expressions of good luck. The night before, the few up that late had pulled themselves out of their preoccupations, had circled her, talking round the horrifying prospect of a prison sentence ahead. She had been touched at their concern and so had not expressed her lack of interest in the whole affair, nor her belief in the vagaries of luck thankfully out of her hands. She was legally guilty (the wording of the offence had been avoided by all) but since the events leading to her arrest had had the mechanical workings of inevitability, she could not feel moral guilt. In her stern new guise, she tried whenever possible to avoid sentimentality.

But now Laura knew that for these same patients, after the initial expressions of shock and outrage, routine would soon settle and she would be forgotten. Were she indeed to suffer violent indignities in prison, no one would know about it. Last night, gratitude had pulled her irresistibly back and then back again towards their concern. But now she was free. Eventually, time would establish its rigid structure again but in the meantime, she could float aimlessly in this void – no sex, no gratitude, no friends, no family, no obligation. She lay down on the plastic mattress of the holding cell.

The door was unlocked and in the entrance Dr Wallace stood uncertain. He came in, leaving the door open slightly.

There was a shrilly clanging bell outside and an officer's face appeared by his side.

'Do you mind? I'll have to ask you to go in or leave. Shouldn't take long . . .'

He looked absolutely startled at the faces looking towards him for evidence of comprehension and answered vaguely, 'No – not at all . . .'

He stepped inside and the door was banged shut and locked.

'Do you want to sit down?'

She sat back down on the plastic bed, indicating its furthest corner. Far too intimate for his liking, he had no option but to comply, since it was he maintaining the illusion of ease.

'You'll have to get used to such proceedings I'm afraid.'

'I would imagine.'

'Eighteen months . . . You'll almost certainly only serve six.'

'Yes.'

They both nodded and stared at the silent room politely.

She thought of his enthusiasm and though in some ways she understood that they both wanted this meeting to be over, she tried again since they had time to fill.

'You were saying – evil?'

But it would have been highly indiscreet in these circumstances, since she was about to be surrounded by violent and noisy candidates of an all too real variety.

'It's a very difficult description.'

As he continued with vague protests of inconclusive evidence, she understood his objections and didn't pursue the subject. Although it was annoying since there was little else to talk about.

At last the door opened with the same chirpy head peering through, officially apologetic. He rose briskly, looking at the light which was following the door's progress.

'Well, I hope you get along all right.'

'Thank you!'

He left, pausing in the doorway, satisfaction of duty radiating out of his raised hand.

Chapter Thirty-one

It was said of the woman with whom she was to share the cell that her cunt stank. Laura was informed of this characteristic her first afternoon in G wing, having been moved up following a week in the holding wing. It was put in this graphic way by a curious observer, Carol, who pushed herself in an affable way from one side of the open door to the other, before moving aside contemptuously to allow access to Sheila the very woman concerned. The officer following behind closed the door. Laura understood that Carol wasn't alone in wishing Sheila ill, because she had airs, and was mad. She belonged in the mad wing, but that was full and she wasn't a danger. Now Laura sat on the bottom bed and watched as Sheila folded her tracksuit trousers with some energy, but as the door was unlocked with the arrival of the evening meal, the accusation was called out again in passing.

'Dirty cunt!'

They ignored this and the door was locked again to silence. Laura disliked the word cunt when used in the context of this, its original meaning. It repulsed her and put her off her food. And eating the cauliflower cheese here in the room, with those useless wide legs dropping down heavily from the bed above – dangling would have been too light a word. Dangling, yes, that brought her back to the very subject she had been trying to avoid in her head. But in spite of the all too evident annoyances – the constant urban soul music outside, the constant shouted jokes, and now the literary chat she was forced to send up to her indifferent and invisible cell mate to compensate for the cruelty and to be polite, Laura knew herself to be remarkably happy in her new surroundings. She felt alive, relaxed and at home. The damp, the hastily conceived colour, and the fat girls quite unaware of modish aspiration – out in the exercise yard, laughing and pushing each other and decked out garishly in mauve and pale blue. The smell too, everyone being cool, sneering and jigging to a tough beat – quite unaware of better worlds, larger and more demanding. Nothing could drag her down from the level of contentment and purpose on which this journey had launched her. Within this meagre vessel, she may have been all at sea, but it was just where she wanted to be, even now, with this malodorous inhabitant above her, snoring and rumbling around.

That night a dream came to her of her father. He was dead and they were in a motel together, she had driven them both there, with bright talk to confuse his lack of animation. In the room, he looked like disintegrating blancmange sitting there, and she asked if perhaps he would like her to get him a change of clothes? He smelt bad but also had on most unattractive and common garments. As she passed the indifferent lobby staff, she felt that they would have no idea of his actual past, his grandeur. She felt bad, realising that she had brought him to a cheaper than usual motel, she would have been loath to drag him past the reception area of her usual expensive choice and back in the room, she tried to talk up the convenience of the place to disguise this. But he was talking, or trying to – but no, he was crying.

The sun the next morning, though providing no heat, transformed the room through the bars and the thin curtains; suddenly, it had the thin neatness of suburbia.

By the third week, Laura was given a privileged job in the gardens. There, she tended to the roses in the care of an officer whose love for her flowers led to a welcome lack of interest in her female charges. She worked side by side with an East Anglian burglar, Sarah, who today was wearing the T-shirt she'd designed, 'to hell with w –'. This last word was covered up with a sewn-on pink patch, in temporary obedience to decorous prison rules.

'Mmmm – "working"?'

'No, girl – no!'

They worked well together; Sarah talked about the African inmates with something like the puzzlement of a hen-pecked anthropologist. She rather admired Laura's scarcely mentioned liberal views and liked her too for her shared avoidance of sentimental analysis. As long as they followed the officer's gardening suggestions, and showed an occasional burst of enthusiasm, Miss Dean left them alone. This diligence and vision had created a maze of brilliant rosebushes, which dazzled and startled the eyes of those turning the corner from the administration offices. It would have taken a cruel and pedantic critic to have spoiled her satisfaction by pointing out that the site of this garden paradise left something to be desired, situated as it was, away from the window view of any of the inmates. The only prisoners to benefit were those who could peer from the passing van windows for one brief flash on their way to court, and those, like Laura now, trusted enough to help out in the fresh air.

Sometimes, as she worked, she thought of Christopher, and when she did so it was with an unsettling feeling of there being unfinished business – and with regret. It was clear that she had behaved badly. The letter she planned to write to him was in her mind but also, more selfishly, a painting of his, *Morocco 1960*. Whenever she tried to hustle herself back into the appropriate preparation for amends to be made, this painting appeared – the bland white face on the grey pillow, the Moorish architecture just reflected in the mirror, the blue and white blinds blowing out . . .

Although Laura knew that at least a third, or perhaps a larger percentage of her recent symptoms sprang from lack of sleep, this logical deduction didn't cancel the feelings of foreboding. She felt certain, the sun now burning on her hands, that this imbalance in her stomach and head must be the beginning of the illness that would be the beginning of the end. And as she made conversation with Sarah, Laura's mind doggedly added up the evidence to support this unwelcome verdict. There were the furtive little fixes, pushed into her veins with no time for even cursory hygiene. There were the gathering number of acquaintances who had disappeared off the scene, leaving only the terrible legend of their having received the doomsday verdict. And there were these symptoms – shoulder ache, nausea and trembling hands, forced into stillness so as to cut the correct dead heads off the roses, diagonally as demonstrated.

She knew she was not, like the subject of the painting, dying in a foreign land; in spite of its incongruous setting this garden was clearly English. But she remembered Christopher's explanation of that trip, as she lay indifferently beside him in his bed one afternoon, his description of the girl's complaints of fatigue and nausea, that had grown gradually less insistent with the foreboding that the increase of the symptoms brought on. By the end, he had said, in order to persuade herself that this was merely a tiresome form of extreme travel sickness – she had stopped saying anything – hoping that with her silence that the ancient local gods of approaching death would lose interest and move on. And so she had lain there, until the day came when a move to the local hospital was unavoidable, her health so crumpled away that the administrative difficulties and lack of privacy therein had made no inroads into her normally fastidious nature.

Laura remembered her conventionally sympathetic response coming as Christopher had answered her question as to how the story ended. He had then risen from the bed, wound the rather short towel round himself and had edged out of the room, not too sad evidently, since she heard his coffee-making noises and he had eventually brought a cup in to her. In deference to his reawakened grief, she had not requested the usual glass of champagne.

And all around them, these wretched roses now irritated, just as they had once charmed her with their dispiriting abundance, like children's high spirits. Much as prison suited her, it was hardly a fit place to get ill, to die, causing as it would, no end of bother to officialdom. And this bother, this nuisance factor would be all too visible on their faces in the midst of her worries, intruding into her preparations for the next stage. If she could just hold out till the end of her sentence – the thought of dying then had a bit of a comfortable feel to it, it would be private at least.

'No, cut them, CUT THEM! What's your name?'

'Do you not know my fucking name by fucking now?'

'You are abusing the privilege of working in these gardens –'

'You can shove your pissing gardens up your arse – !'

On a dog-trot journey back along the paths behind the officers manhandling the struggling Sarah, Laura assured the shocked officer time and time again that she quite understood that the lock-up punishment was not directed towards her.

'You like being on your own?'

'It has its advantages.'

Laura's one-time cell mate Femni laughed very heartily. She always was highly amused by Laura and the feeling was reciprocated. Laura had enjoyed their spasmodic chats on royalty, a particular relief after Sheila's careful pretensions. Femni had read aloud the letters received from her family in Africa, no response had been required, certainly not sympathy. However, since having been moved again a month ago from their shared cell to this single one Laura luxuriated in the even greater ease of solitude.

'Here are your letters. Ver-ry popular!'

It was true that even after having served three months of her sentence, she still received many letters. Some of them, from the rehabilitation centre patients were full of factual good cheer, others from the outside, frivolous. These last were more enjoyable to read and more taxing to reply to, since they demanded wit. But this? At the top of the envelope, above the handwriting she knew so well, was the scrawled official demand, that the name of the sender be provided. At that moment, one of the officers came by with a clipboard. Laura provided Christopher's name and she hurried it in and left her locked up again.

She was disconcerted, she had thought that she had relinquished the demands, advantageous and otherwise, of Christopher's celebrated company. She took the letter out of the open envelope with some foreboding. Its contents were sparse, but certainly its arrival signalled acceptance and forgiveness. He had included a reproduction of *Early Birds* that had so charmed her once and did so again now. It was something about the ungainly figure jumping in the air and above him the all-over-the-place flapping birds and only in one low corner the toad like a piece of rubbish. She propped it against her notice board.

The letter she had been putting off writing to him would have been difficult; she would have tried for some sort of dignified atonement. But now she wrote back immediately, and quite confidently she knew her letter to be rich with peculiar incident. She knew that his curiosity, more directly expressed than most, would be tickled by the more grotesque illustrations of female delinquency, her rich store having been increased even by the new job in the library that exposed her to every wing.

She told of one of the angels in the recent nativity play, who not content with starting a fire inside the bus shelter, had dug a hole in her arm and filled it with green ink. She did not include in this letter the murderous crime of the other angel, also of course from the mad wing, spelt out with graphic disgust by her neighbour Maria. She wanted to avoid any sort of relish in this fanatical hallucinatory baptism. It was a crime that in spite of her interest, disturbed her. To make up for that omission, she did include the lunchtime masturbator's antics, up against her window with a toothbrush, although she also felt a certain reluctance here, knowing that he would find it sexually stimulating, and it was not.

The letter had the effect she had intended. Christopher's

mind was crammed with little moving figures, little wayward females. He liked to believe the worst. It amused him, it fitted his philosophy and it comforted him.

Later that day, he described some of the incidents to Jane who laughed. She felt bored at the signs of renewed interest. She need not have worried. Laura's sights had moved far beyond a return to that particular past, too well explored now. Trampled down now, in fact, to a level where all light and shade had been crushed away. Left now was a prestigious site no doubt, but one lacking the necessary spark, the myth of the undiscovered.

He wrote back, suggesting she make a record of her experiences. She was astounded. Christopher, more than anyone she had met, loathed the idea that creativity (even that word caused him to shrink with disgust) was sitting there waiting to be tapped with a bit of self care and imagination indulgently pursued. Of course, he hardly bothered to pursue this argument, since all around it was being ignored, but the products of this appallingly fruitful activity sometimes brought to his attention, commanded his most violent diatribes in that direction.

It was a line that Laura agreed with. If not the best, why do it at all? From the start Christopher had raised art to the highest possible level; initially few had recognised it, but even fewer created its equal. And the majority of the world should refrain from attempting it at all.

His arguments had been one of the reasons she had not taken seriously the constant refrain that she should write something. She had only supposed it to be directed at her for lack of any other suggestion. And as for the rigorous application needed, she had none of it. She liked reading and was fairly imaginative. That was it.

She lay back down on the bed, stared at the ceiling. For once there were no troubling thoughts of guilt at her own futile existence. All she need do was wait for the day of release, three months off if she was granted parole. And after all the treatment centre's probing, it was a lazy relief that a prison sentence was the weakest conduit towards truthful self-analysis she had yet found. Nothing needed or could be done in its comfortable miasma of boredom, except wait and dream of the glorious future that would begin on day one of release. She couldn't help the thought that inside this artificially adapted society, time was managed perfectly, entirely directed to a specific moment in the future when real life would start again.

Chapter Thirty-two

The girl who had met Laura on the first day on the wing, Carol, having been freed on parole, was back having broken the terms of her release with a fight in a pub. Placed on another wing, she always greeted Laura as an old friend when they met, and now was trying to attract her attention, to make her boredom evident, since the creative assignment was no longer living up to her initial expectations. She had been loudly amused at first by the idea of 'trapped' as a theme for an essay, picture or poem. The teacher, Mr Saunders, had started with the cut roses in the glass container, but had unhurriedly progressed to a large reproduction of Michelangelo's *Captive*. Holding it up to the still indulgent room, he had explained that the artist here had not needed to be explicit, to tell a story as such. Even the difference between the finished figure and the rough stone from which it seemed to be struggling was powerful enough a contrast, that the theme of entrapment was clear. Did they agree? And there were a few nods, difficult to read whether of indifference or agreement. In the pause that followed, Mr Saunders turned to pin the reproduction up next to the blackboard, explaining at the same time that there would be no need for self-consciousness, that no one need show their efforts unless they felt like it. He added the ubiquitous assurance that, of course, any that were up to sharing their work, would find their courage greatly appreciated. But it seemed unlikely in those first few moments of silence and bewilderment that there would be anything at all to examine in the near future.

Laura stared at the roses from the grounds which had frozen into interesting positions in their jar, as false as paper. Was it that they would come to life by being drawn? What an absurdity! And the table too, and the jam jar, dully and suitably in the background – Laura daydreamed. And looking up, the objects were decorative again. Continuing with her efforts, she felt disinclined towards accuracy with all its little faults. The wishy-washy result was artistic – she was quite prepared to defend its abstraction with a meaningful silence, but she had no need, Mr Saunders passed on with a disappointing 'good'.

To her side, Carol, having despised the initial lack of initiative, had taken her pen and had started to write immediately. But like many others before her, evidently she had found that word after word written down took her further away from her randomly creative high spirits that had thrown up such confident bursts of imagery on first hearing the idea.

After some moments of trying, she put down her pen noisily, resentful that the rest of the room didn't follow her lead. She noticed that even her old adversary Sheila, two desks in front, was writing absorbedly. Laura, too, had been surprised by her one-time cell mate's absorption. But Carol hadn't lost her entertainer's touch and stood up with a loud yawn. A little attention coming her way, she sauntered across the room and then casually snatched Sheila's effort.

'Let's have a look then!'

Turning to the now receptive room, she waved above Sheila's ineffectual arms this paper in a clear notice to all that it was about to be read aloud.

Out of the corner of her eye, Laura saw that Mr Saunders had noticed Carol's forbidden act of pillage, but for such a brief second that he had evidently persuaded himself he had seen nothing. There was always noise and movement in the prison education rooms, such a class could hardly achieve the silence of a normal adult education course in the circumstances such as they were here. He wandered with assumed indifference to where the middle-aged Indian woman next to Laura was labouring with genteel despair over her essay, which almost certainly conventionally centred on her sorrow at being away from her family back in Delhi. Having obtained her permission with an enquiring look, he read it over her shoulder in order that he might encourage and point the way forward in quiet voice.

Laura assumed that had his conscience or authority asked him what the hell he was up to, he would have replied in his quiet ineffectual voice that problems often solved themselves, interfering in his opinion only increased the likelihood of trouble. Now he pointed to a grammatical error, explaining quietly to the frantically nodding head that it was unimportant in itself, but its correction might add to what was a very promising start. Meanwhile, there was growing commotion in the furthest corner of the room, giving the lie to his pacifist's theory. Carol was fending off the indignant arms of the author still.

She shouted the start in loud and clear tones of derision. 'My exhaustion traps me!'

Having enchanted the room into silence, she began again with academic precision.

'My exhaustion traps me. Like an overworked vagina, my muscles are just unable to let go into release. The build-up is very strong but that just causes greater exhaustion. It just isn't possible unless I use my own false manipulation to come to an unsatisfactory conclusion. Not at all at the right time or place, but it does bring a sort of closure to the ongoing event . . .'

Mr Saunders had been forced to notice this by now obvious breach of confidentiality, but unable to stop it without a great deal of fuss ensuing, he had waited with the raised hand of objection until the reading was over. And he was surprised into courage by the silence of its reception and his own amazement.

He marched over, took the paper and handed it back to the seated Sheila, saying, 'I know you had not given your permission for this to be read, and that it was wrong for

174

Carol to do so, but now we've heard it, I have to say, it has real potential for literary merit.'

Rather than his words, it was his tone of authority that led to an outbreak of jeering and whistles. The women had disliked hearing the piece; it had been disgusting and unusual. Carol too, had been disconcerted by the silence that had greeted her finish, but rather than be annoyed with Mr Saunders's audacity, she took on to herself the acclaim that was now ringing round the room.

Laura was the most disconcerted of all of them. This was an original piece, but she might have expected originality of thought from a lunatic. But also it contained some ideas that were worthy of study. She wanted to know the source of this appalling inspiration.

The time had come for the class to end. As they all filed out, Laura asked permission of Sheila if she could borrow the piece to read again in her room.

Not wanting to look at it straight away, Laura had put it under her letters, but the next afternoon she got it out and read it many times and, eventually her own enthusiasm having been dulled with repetition, she was able to persuade herself that it lacked originality.

And now, lying immobile on the bed, Laura looked at her fingers, so fat and grublike; they should be holding the fucking pencil and using it to drag up some goddamned originality from her own gorgeous little anecdotes of the past.

She thought of Tom's letter, received two weeks ago. Remembering his stilted phrases, it was strange to her that she had ever felt that he was glamorous; for a moment she had mistaken his name for an obscure patient in rehab, and had replied eventually with the same careless courtesies as if it had been.

It was intolerably boring in prison. Laura got up and gazed out of the window. In the distance the waving sycamore leaves appeared over the top of the wall like green paws drawn by children. Her hands grew increasingly itchy from irritation; the repetitive humorous calls, one to another and back again.

There was a knock on her open door – 'Do you want to come to association?' But the attractions of prison had all but disappeared. And she indeed felt dismal at the thought of another afternoon of watching modern-day sheriffs chasing cars over the Texan back roads to the accompaniment of yells and fiddle music. But she left her cell and sat, on the heavy plastic chair with the others, smiling appreciatively at the screen, in order to appreciate even more, the solitude that would return again in less than an hour.

Carol, seeing her, screeched a chair heavily over towards hers and sat down momentarily.

'Oh my God, was my shouting disturbing you?'

'Not at all, I was just thinking.'

'What – about your boyfriend?'

'My ex-boyfriend.'

'Miss him, do you?'

'No.'

'Go on – miss his good loving – admit it, girl, you do!!'

'I admit nothing – !!

Carol rolled back, laughing towards the officer standing waiting to collect the group leaving for the exercise yard. She stood up, taking Laura with her, talking for all to hear. But Laura's thoughts turned to the evening meal coming – nowadays, she was less intent on thinness, but before release she wanted to return somewhere towards her one-time figure to show the world she meant business . . .

'. . . But they have to be nice, too. That's right, girl?'

'Yes.'

'And he wasn't nice to you?'

'Nice enough. Just a bit of a cunt.'

Carol dropped her hold on Laura, started shaking her head with judicious disapproval as they moved off.

'No, no, no – you shouldn't use words like that. It don't sound good coming from you.'

'But these are the words I use in everyday life!'

'No, it don't sound good.'

They reached the entrance to the exercise yard, but now the prison officer's raised hand held them back to allow the little procession of the segregated rule 43's sexual abusers to get by. They plodded past, as if animals in the desert, one deliberate step after the other, their surroundings apparently quite without interest even when potentially dangerous. Even Laura's known and exceptionally courteous presence was ignored, that in their weekly library visits drew them to her fascinated, slyly fingering the recommendations. Laura was allowed to indulge her liberal views since her status was acceptably odd, but she too found repellent, those bloodless hands inching over the cellophane book jackets that had committed or colluded with such acts of cruelty, that their owners were now not fit for human society.

'Fucking animals, aren't they?'

'No.'

'No?'

'All right – come on, inside!'

Once in the yard, they wandered around the grass of the yard in desultory patterns, Carol talking about a planned get-together organised by Linda, another woman due to be released in the following month. Carol was pleased to have been invited, and kept eliciting signs of equal enthusiasm from Laura who was happy to comply. This particular yard was small but had gradients and one corner was the mad wing that was occasionally entertaining to those passing close enough to it.

'Hey! Hello! Hellohhello helloaahh.'

Having been heard, Miss Halley doubled up then rose and continued towards them. This particular officer was rarely seen above the speed of a stroll, but now she ran again, brandishing the flowers ahead of her with as much delicacy as she could manage considering the urgency of her mission and this unnatural pace. She bent down again comically as she got to them, then straightened with her breath back, to explain her previous night's drunkenness and the mistake that had meant that Laura's flowers had sat for a day in the office, undelivered so to speak.

'I've got them now, that's fine.'

Laura took the flowers; they were from her mother. They were expensive, sort of orange daisies, which looked commonplace. As they walked on, Laura held them as inconspicuously as she could, considering they were the subject of Carol's attempts to corral Laura into a general criticism of the prison system.

'And they'll fucking die not in water now!'

'No they'll be all right for the time we'll be out here.'

The arsonist was at her post at the basement window, offering up sex for fifty pence, and they paused so that she could receive the usual yelled reply from Carol, of overcharging and being disgusting. With a lunatic's perception, the arsonist responded with sentimentality. She reached her fingers out towards the flowers, recalling, with a semblance of dignity, childhood country hedges, stuffed with orange berries. Laura faltered, then, stepping a little out of her companion's range, handed one of the stems to the hands grasping out of the window.

The face looked disgusted at the gift. Then the hands, having grasped how to manoeuvre the flower inside by dint of clasping it in one not both, took it to the mouth. One petal was nibbled off delicately, then another and then the whole mess crammed in. They left her chewing like a fish, mouth open and closing with mechanical efficiency.

Laura blushed and shrugged. She was handling it well she thought, as if she had either sought the hysterical delight of her companion or as if she appreciated herself, the slightly embarrassing metaphor of something or other, enacted before their eyes.

Chapter Thirty-three

'How long since you had sex then?'

'About a year.'

'Fucking hell!'

'But how long were you inside?'

'About six months.'

Russ let go of her shoulder, evidently celibacy rather revolted him.

'What did you do in there without it? Mas-tur-bating all day long like the rest of them!'

Laura smiled – she wasn't going to be embarrassed by his insistent attempts to reveal what he clearly imagined was her upper-class prudery. She had been out of prison for only three weeks now, but this freedom celebration was proving to be more turgid than any captivity. There were five of them in the party, coming and going from their table and back again. It was clear, whenever she provided any interest at all, that her oddity produced irritable embarrassment rather than the amiable curiosity she had grown used to over the last months inside. But Carol's boyfriend was fat and kind – although his inquisitive well meaning was on the heavy side.

'– but if you're a girl, you don't have the same urges – isn't that right?'

Laura answered with laconic disinterest – she was damned if she would bow to the pressure to conform to the conventions of this amphetamine-fuelled group who were evidently finding her wanting.

'I don't suppose there's much difference between men and women fundamentally.'

'Not much difference!'

Russ's eyes swept up his audience for their equal disbelief.

'You really have been away from dick for too long!'

They talked about which club to start off with next, and the argument left Laura able to smile towards her mineral water with the pretence of equal high spirits. The question settled, the talk turned to child molesters and Laura remained quiet. It was pointed out that she didn't believe in capital punishment and this galvanised Russ again.

'My friend, yeah? He –'

(There was laughter at some clumsiness from Jed climbing over the bench to get to the bar.)

'– He –'

Now he turned and stared at Laura, less sincerity evident than the cruel curiosity of a child observing the workings of nature.

'Got himself into a cell with one – broke every finger of his hand – one for every child he touched.'

But a response was not required. His humorous high spirits returned with Jed's arrival, back with more spilt drinks.

'FUCKING CUNT! – Look at you!'

Drearily, having sat in the tube and then having walked through the park, Laura decided to take advantage of the advertised early opening hours of the Natural History Museum. She felt that the informatively laid out origins of life would distract her after her failed attempt to shine.

Alone in her prison room, she had anticipated that prospective party with something like pride, the pride of belonging to a dangerous gang. She had boasted of it casually in her letters, as if bored by the prospect.

Now, she wandered into the advertised room that had – having been shipped from its home in New York – a great replicated blue whale hanging from the ceiling. She looked at it, trying to substitute its strange appearance for the flashing oval night-club table, the last gathering point of all curious revellers. She ignored the only other person in the room, a small boy with red hair looking her way. He was wearing a marmoset backpack and eating a Curly Wurly with shy greed. But soon he came and stood near her.

Finally he asked, 'Do you know what whales do?'

'No.'

Her spirits were sinking. She knew she should be enchanted by his quirkiness, but instead, she felt oppressed.

'They make this noise, listen.'

She held the headset reluctantly to her ears and heard the underwater piping of innumerable new age treatment rooms.

'Yes, that's lovely.'

She handed back the headset, but something about her reaction had embarrassed him. He looked down.

She asked him, as if in contemplation, 'Do you think they *are* talking to one another?'

'Of *course!*'

Perhaps the tartness of his reply reflected his humiliation. It was good revenge because Laura did feel a berk.

He announced casually, 'I have to go.'

He couldn't have made his disinterest clearer, wandering off in sidling fashion. And she had to go too; she couldn't hang around for ever in those great halls.

And so she returned to a silent breakfast at her mother's flat, and this one, like all the other days, swelled and bloated out repulsively with lack of use. Vivienne found her presence infuriating! They had never spent this much time in each other's company, and apparently for good reason. They had covered the subject of prison on the first night out, and with dignity; Vivienne had then felt it the moment to express and describe her own fears that had lasted the length of Laura's incarceration. But neither wanted to broach the subject that had, through time, grown massively like a ghost with raised arms – her abuse. But Laura's perpetual silence now rendered awkwardness quite obsolete.

'Is that situation with the man at Kentigern still on your mind?'

'No.'

Laura got up from the table, took her glass to the kitchen. But her return found Vivienne still sitting, the look of impatient anguish on her face.

'Because, you seem to find it impossible to do anything.'

Laura's silence created further certainty.

'So I just assumed it might have something to do with that.'

'No.'

She left the table, feeling sick.

And in her room, the sickness grew – against all recent training towards practical positivity, she felt the overwhelming urge to imagine her mother wretched and dead.

And the days went on – she was wild with inadequacy!

She knocked at the lawyer's door, and he called her in. During her rehabilitation phase, her flat had been sold and the little coloured drawing too, in order that her legal and medical costs might be paid. Those in charge had quite underestimated the value of both, quite understandably, given the perilous nature of the financial circumstances and the need for quick action. Mr Rawson, the lawyer, had not concluded that his judgement was faulty; he had described the work to his wife as an indulgence of a now famous painter, quite without merit on its own terms. But the latter had fetched an inconceivably high sum and now there was quite a considerable amount left over.

'Perhaps I might give some of it to charity?'

He stared at her with dislike over his erroneously benevolent owl glasses.

'I think you will need all the money quite as much. After all . . .'

(But her face still reflected bland incomprehension.)

'It's not everyone who will want to employ you now – and you don't have that much experience of the . . . "world of work" . . .'

*

182

That night she visited Christopher. He was amused by her gangster night out – but not that much. She told him of her hatred of living with Vivienne (she knew how to pander to his taste). But he seemed not to take the bait. He seemed pre-occupied; she knew that downward look of agitation well. But his agitation was for her.

He turned. 'You have to find some employment – a class in something, education – anything!'

He illustrated this unusually direct advice with a story from the Bible. As he began, she thought that this return to his circuitous methods would produce a drifting narrative that would leave her having to make the links, should she feel willing. But it was quite direct – God, infuriated by the bore-dom of his rescued and now stranded tribe, ordered as work, the weaving of baskets – futile though the finished product would be on that interminable desert plain!

Christopher then offered her the old job as artist's model.

'I accept!'

But her droll glee led to the erotic movements for which she felt nothing but revulsion.

'I'm not sleeping with him any more.'

She had expected something from her parole officer Graham; some expression of gratification. But he sat, a polite expres-sion on his face, waiting for the next part, the important aspect of the revelation.

Finally he asked, 'And does this cause difficulties within the relationship?'

'But there is no relationship. I'm just modelling for him.'

Graham nodded.

As had been stipulated within the terms of her parole, they met once a week. It seemed in some ways that Laura had more rigour towards the demands of authority than he, since he occasionally advised a relaxation of the rules.

Prior to her release, he had made an appointment to inspect her mother's flat, the officially declared parole accommodation, but had done so with an amused air. Arriving, Vivienne had nervously laughed along with him, but she found herself unable to accommodate his evident worldliness. She had vaguely expected a resentful white representative of official-dom with a timid regional accent.

He had sat, drinking his coffee, and had talked of his roots – he had left Africa at the age of four. Now his parents lived there again, in Kenya. Bewildered still by his amiable presence she had thought to tell him of she and Charles's one-time friendship with King Freddie, unsurprisingly making a little more of their association than perhaps was quite accurate. He had understood the reasoning behind this particular refer-ence, but this sort of racial categorising was too subtle to be offensive; in his job as parole officer he was privy to more accurate aims.

Now he asked Laura, 'You don't seem to talk much of your mother.'

'No.'

'Is it working out – your staying in her flat?'

'No.'

Laura knew by now that Graham was far too sophisticated to impose the rules set by the prison authorities. Nor did he wholeheartedly endorse the treatment centre's simplistic philosophy, but made it plain that he would not dispute any form of effective support. His face remained kindly and impassive if ever she allowed the fervency of her new-found moralistic belief to slip through in her remarks to him.

Now she ventured, 'You know, I would have preferred to return to my old flat.'

'On your own?'

'Yes.'

'But didn't you say that you were glad to leave it with all its associations?'

'I know. I was repeating what I'd been taught in treatment.'

And never had the thought of the drab dark flat seemed so lovely; it had been hers after all! And, after all, associations, meaning surely memory, were what she was made up of? The brick by brick foundations determining the unsteady shape of the present – and even some sort of future ready to soar into existence? Oh but these little thoughts didn't last long – she blushed to remember them once the fit of 'stinking thinking' had passed and she was back within the safety of the well-fenced fold.

'I think you'd better look into renting a place on your own.'

'Really?'

'Really.'

'Even though the terms of the parole . . .'

'I don't think you'll be clapped back in irons for that.'

He tapped his hands on the desk a couple of times.

'We're going to have to finish early. I'm taking my parents to the theatre – in fact –'

He got up to peer through the frosted glass pane – and before opening the door, turned with raised eye brow to include Laura in a wry appreciation of parental punctuality . . .

'Here already – good good!'

They rose from their plastic seats, and shook her hand as he checked his next day's appointments with the receptionist.

At one point he interrupted their chat about plays to say, 'You know, Laura's parents knew the Kabaka – King Freddie.'

They were politely interested.

'And did you meet him?'

'Yes – I liked him very much. He told us about his pet bears.'

They laughed with loud, slow, clearly announced laughter – Ha, ha ha. Not false but restrained, as if their thoughts were some immeasurable distance away.

Chapter Thirty-four

The creative writing teacher, Stephen, had glasses and a sandy face. Laura liked his bemused Highland accent and his manner of folding himself over into modest but assured reproof when it was necessary. Continuing his talk on cliché, he said, 'Now. Perhaps you have seen or read these famous works too often, they have turned into kitsch, the yellow bower of flowers, the dark-haired housewife with the suggestive smile – giving you what message . . . ?'

'To slap the smile off her face?'

He laughed, but even his reluctance to concur was flattering to the speaker, a young man of skeletal intensity and an abysmal confidence in his feeble efforts.

'I don't think they deserve such punishment, such extreme reaction, *necessarily*. But by all means . . .'

Laura began – writing in pencil in her plain paper notebook:

'It's difficult to write a memoir of childhood and to be honest, it annoys me to have to try.'

But back in her narrow room, she crossed out the 'to be honest' remembering the humorous advice of her old lover, who had leaned over her earlier, reading her words, his skin disconcertingly grey and badly fitting like a cheap handbag. She lay down on the bed and held the notebook open above her head like a cathedral. She thought about the sex she'd been having recently, in fact that very morning. She supposed it to be about as good as she'd ever imagined it to be. There was no way of telling; she had never gone into that much detail growing up. Generally speaking, she'd seen sex as a crude method of evaluating her success in the world. Certainly she had had some moments of

186

wanting it, but that had been sublimated now into a more
romantic ideal . . .

Stephen read it over her shoulder and laughed.

'Carry on – I like the start!'

They all went to the pub after the class had finished. Seeing Laura sitting somewhat apart, he wandered up.

'Water only?'

'I'm a recovering alcoholic.'

'Oh.'

He sat down next to her.

'It doesn't matter if it takes time to read anything out loud. It *is* nerve wracking.'

'I prefer to write for myself only.'

She told him of the incidents that had led to her sobriety, including her arrest and imprisonment. She sweated doing so, but to his credit, he seemed not to be too excited by the presence of a bona fide underdog. Instead he laughed, and she did too. He had a habit of opening his hands into Josephine Baker starfishes, she'd noticed this trait in the class. He looked down at them, and closed his fingers again. They talked of music and by his preferences, she realised he was nearer her age than she had imagined, authority had added superfluous years.

Chapter Thirty-five

In the old days, Charles's doctors had been of the grander Harley Street variety, the sort who would have quite likely been members of his club. The manner of their delivery had always been reassuringly throwaway, and the ailments they attended infrequent and routine.

But his life and financial circumstances having changed, his most recent doctor worked out of an office in Fulham. Charles still felt it preferable that he see a London practitioner. And although Dr Baring's hearty familiarity jarred his nerves, Charles's superstitious belief that London doctors held the keys to greater knowledge than their country counterparts kept him going back. Once he had jocularly prescribed 'perhaps a little less of the gin and tonics' . . . (raising his hand in drinking motion). But he had added 'Oh I know, we have to have a little of what we like at our time of life – that's what I tell my wife . . .' leaving Charles on the train home to wonder what he had actually meant – he had met the wife, a hysterical frowsy drunk.

Today, Charles ran into him in the reception area and Dr Baring had looked angry to see him there so early. He had nodded and hurried into his office with a gesture meaning 'not quite ready'. Later he had opened the door and had beckoned Charles to sit with none of the usual pleasantries concerning the benefits of country life. Instead he had kept his eyes on the notes he had in his hands, had sat and finally looked up somewhat disgusted.

'The results of the tests.'

'Yes. Not good.'

'Not good. No.'

*

That day he was having lunch with Vivienne. Throughout the meal he was quiet but he seemed serene rather than sulky, nodding occasionally and making the correct remarks of interest when she talked of Laura's new rented flat, chuckling at the restrained irritation towards Laura's lack of decorative effort. Towards the end of the meal, as she was returning with the coffee, Charles cleared his throat, said with an embarrassed little smile that he had some bad news to break. Her breath froze in her throat, but she sat down without drama. He told her the medical facts that had been given him that morning.

'Oh, my dear Charles.'

Vivienne did not cry. She had the grace to provide what he wanted, and she knew at that moment what he wanted was stoicism. She made a grab at him and a hug, then left off immediately to pour the coffee.

Later that day, sitting on the train back to the country, he looked out at the increasingly suburban looking countryside, its dark green conifers and unbecoming lanes the reason that he and Jeanette had been able to afford their little bit of land adjoining the house. Suddenly he felt dismayed and resentful that death involved so much added work. As if it wasn't bad enough on its own, he would have to break the news, comfort and deal with Jeanette throughout the coming days. Instead of peaceful relinquishment, lying on his bed like some peasant in his hut surrounded by animals and quite able to cope, he would have to talk and respond, something he had not had to do much of for the past few years. For the last few years he had been bored, a state of mind that he had wished for without putting that name to it. Certainly now it seemed most attractive and unattainable. And to a lesser extent, he would have to deal with Laura's grief. He hoped, but it was just a short thought, that she would be sad.

Charles took another whisky from the drinks tray filled with superfluous bottles – visitors were rare. Removing the bottle revealed the south transept of Kentigern Abbey and he thought of what to say. As he sat with a grunt of satisfaction, Jeanette watched him, asked him questions about his London visit with an oblique air of suspicion. He rose to replenish his drink from time to time, not really answering and only livening up with the terrier's appearance, alert with the frost outside. He put down his finger and the dog brushed past it amusingly as it yearned towards the door, but Jeanette did not respond to his little laugh. He had found another non-dog lover; she treated it with patience and talked to it with clear pronunciation as if to a child.

Now he got up and urged, 'Come on!'

As he opened the french windows, it pushed past him in hooligan fashion. Charles shut the door behind him, watched it run in passionate pursuit, slowing to a listless sniff of one or other of the plant pots. It was well below freezing and the geraniums needed moving to a sheltered spot in case of snow. He dragged them one by one towards the wall of the house then stood back and observed his efforts. The slow moving rings of a bad dream haunted him, but with the tiresome facts in place, he was unable to chivvy himself out of apprehension with the usual sensible rebuke in such circumstances – it may be a premonition, but almost certainly isn't.

Coming in, he described his rescuing of the plants and they sat in silence.

Jeanette never tackled the issue of his drinking directly; instead, she allowed the sight and sound to permeate her thin skin, puff it up sip by sip, until the limit was reached and she was forced to shrivel into collapse. He tremendously disliked this transformation, taking place as usual in the corner of the room. But tonight he had had the means to put a stop to it – this puncture, delivered with slow uncharacteristic cruelty, left her aghast.

The door to the bedroom opened and she came and stood beside him. Then she sat on the bed too, head in hands and he put his arm round her bent shoulders.

'I just hoped – oh God, I just hoped that we'd have some time together down here.'

His earlier presentiment had been accurate; Jeanette was avid for comfort of the least available sort. To compensate for his earlier cruelty, he now felt obliged to spend a great deal of effort on proposing false hope – a suitable punishment to be sure. He disliked the burden of having to add back the layers of possibilities, having had them removed once and for all by force of circumstance. He looked forward to Laura's arrival the next night; he desired rest.

Laura arrived, apparently full of the enthusiasm for the writing course on which she had embarked. Her enthusiasm seemed and indeed was false. She had decided on the train down that it was a suitable subject. But she was already resentful, more than she had realised and their usual blank indifference and conversational substitutes infuriated her suddenly. He was an alcoholic and she was – intolerable!

Charles rose slowly. 'I think I'll have a bath.'

Left alone with Jeanette, there was a silence. Finally Laura stood up with as much amiability as she could muster, stretching as if casual.

'I'll just get a mineral water.'

'There's one there open on the drinks tray.'

Jeanette came and stood beside her and her silence invited enquiry.

'What?'

Charles's heavy tread was suddenly above them, and Jeanette hearing it clasped the table and began to cry, with an agonised motion of dismissal.

Laura, regretting her rudeness, put her hand on Jeanette's arm, suggesting, 'Shall we go to the sitting-room?'

And as they made their way there, a sudden dark sickness had to be smothered. She would know soon enough.

She sat and heard the lead up to the facts. Finally and with some gentleness, Laura spelt out the ultimate scenario when

Jeanette seemed unable to form the words. She felt her strengths could lie in practical truthfulness, but to herself only. Jeanette seemed inclined towards the easing off of the truth, and towards the shading of the harsh edges that implied a get-out.

'But as I was telling Charles last night, there are such good treatments nowadays.'

'That's absolutely right.'

When they heard the sound of Charles coming heavily down the stairs, Laura left the room to meet him. As he reached the bottom step, a rueful smile on his face, she gave him a hug and was surprised to find herself crying just a little as he patted her clumsily on the back.

'Sorry.'

'That's OK.'

As she looked up, she saw that his plain face looked beatifically gratified.

Outside it was icy, earlier it had snowed. Charles and Laura stood side by side in the dark, considering the dilemma of the swan. It stood ungainly and inelegant on the ice of the pond, considering their presence casually. Flattered by their attention it took two flabby steps and at once fell, its wing outstretched to break its fall and then regained its upright position.

Having fetched bread from the kitchen, Laura now threw another trail of bread as a lure, summoning it towards the small pool of unfrozen dark water in which it would be at home. She felt foolish, her city ways and sentimental wish to be friends with animals. Her father standing, his arms hanging down, so sullen and uninterested by her side, perhaps was thinking the same thing.

But suddenly with a lurching effort (perhaps the bread had helped, perhaps not) the swan managed to propel itself enough forward that a splashing fall into the water was inevitable. And at once it was elegantly at home, indeed, mildly surprised at its second leisurely turn, to find them there, watching still.

And in the dark Charles was grinning. She felt the same and they turned back towards the house.

She said, 'Satisfactory.'

'Yes.'

'Do you remember the swan I thought was a ghost?'

But even he was able to make the leap to what other connection that memory had for him. He appreciated her attempts to make it charming. But ghosts weren't his favourite subject now, perhaps since he would soon be of their realm; no longer intrigued and doubtful as to the validity of the uncanny, but part of it.

The next afternoon they rummaged in the boxes in his scarcely used attic office. No one had ever thought to ask what had come of the hopes of his business venture. He did not invite these sorts of practical questions any more; his delicately blown shapes of future fancy had puffed into final evaporation.

'Here's something.'

He held out an old-fashioned packet of Kodak prints. She looked at the selection of photographs that had been piled into this packet, some small black and white, others more recent: she and Martin sharing a sledge, Jeanette thumbs up under a 'Sold' sign, she again as a child, holding the terrier in a fierce grip by the abbey –

'Ah ha!'

He stumbled to his feet, gave her a pile of newspaper. Inside this wrapping was a plate, a reproduction of the triumph of Galatea. On it, surrounded by bright-blue water, were numerous cities of water. Beside the shell carriage of the heroine, swam fish and tritons, turning over in the blue water and blowing trumpets.

'I love it!'

Laura felt bewildered by the succession of feelings and

memories. It was disturbing to realise that with this evidence of his paternal involvement, her grief would have to deepen. From having felt reconciled and full of practical plans, she now felt bereft at the thought of the months ahead, all leading inexorably to his death. She had reconciled herself to the somewhat convenient belief of childhood abandonment and alcoholism untreated.

'Thank you!'

She turned to see him blushing at her pleasure. She took the plate to her room, and there she sat down. Confusedly she wondered whether this was a manifestation of love, this emotion struggling and beating to announce its pitiful and messy message in her stomach and heart.

She turned the plate over and brushed into the waste-paper basket the great tangled web of dirt still clinging with a couple of determined strands. It crossed her mind that her indifference to the spidery dust was a sign that she too was nearer the grave, but, of course, it was just as likely that she had more important things on her mind than disgust at webbing.

Chapter Thirty-six

Christopher's show was inspiring such a volume of diverse review that it would have been hard even for his keenest detractors to misrepresent its importance. Now critics swept past the controversial nudes without a glance – straight to cautious appraisal of the first and last works – a miracle to have a master in these mediocre times!

Laura had not been able to make the opening party – she had explained to Christopher that she was visiting Charles who was unwell. Although he asked for no details, Christopher perhaps intuited that Charles's wish for status would flare up again in illness – a grasp at the basest survival instinct. He asked if she would like it to be arranged that she go with him to the show in the hours before it opened to the public?

Charles accepted the offer with enthusiasm. He wanted to go on outings that they could both share. Walking along the South Bank, he seemed determined to please, laughing and making an effort to respond to her comments. She couldn't help noticing that his teeth through his open mouth looked grey and loose or was she imagining it?

They gave their names and then stood in the first room, looking for directions. They wandered through the rooms that showed Christopher's early works. The energy and charm made her smile, but apparently they had not much effect on Charles. They moved on, looked at the infant Tom squalling on his mother's breast, a smaller painting than she had remembered it in the Kielders' library.

In that room were two portraits of Angus too, a head and a nude. In this first, his fleshy mouth hung to one side, his blue eyes bulging – his face looked every bit the sort on whom fame would confound the conventional by settling. In the nude, he lay full length, his hand flopped on his pale stomach.

Off it, in a tiny room on its own, was the masterpiece, the grappling men. Laura passed by quickly without entering the room; superstitiously she wished it to retain the potency of memory. Finally they came to the contemporary room, stood in front of her portrait. It was the first time she had seen it framed and official. Charles looked at it, made appreciative noises. It was easy to find the correct remarks to make; it was harmoniously constructed and obscurely coloured.

'Shall we go on?'

But in the next room was the monumental elephant painting and Charles relaxed. He was dying, he could afford to lower himself into the cosy dark vat of the philistine. He smiled at Laura apologetically.

'My favourite!'

'Yes, it is nice.'

The gallery had now opened its doors and there were already many enthused visitors in front of the popular painting. He joined their ranks, making way for a Chinese couple holding up their mildly interested child for a look. Suddenly the crowd moved on and he and Laura were able to stand alone. And together they looked one more time at the little starfish shape of the pink trunk arching round into the frame again, unnaturally posed underneath that grey and green expanse of mottled hide and dark eye of absolute incomprehension.

Chapter Thirty-seven

Jane, finally having had enough of Paul's second-rate snob-bery, had announced at the end of a dinner party, when asked if she had any plans for that week, that her only plan was to leave him. He had fulfilled his pompous reputation and had merely thrown aside his napkin, risen slowly and left the room as if his only cares were ones of taste. He had learned his assimilating lessons too well and now was situated at a level above the unknown mentors from whom he had under-stood that dignity and indifference walked side by side.

This had been the version she had relayed to Christopher, omitting the tears that had come later from the dissolved figure in the green armchair.

And with an unexpected burst of love, she and Christopher had decided to marry. They would have to wait up to a year for the divorce to be complete, but uncharacteristically Christo-pher had seemed enthusiastic at the idea of Jane's brother Archie hosting a dinner party to celebrate their engagement. Archie had never liked Paul, but this gesture had been offered with the shy terseness of one expecting a rebuff. But neither of them having children Christopher felt that it would be a sub-stitute family occasion, with all the attendant nuisance value. And in the careless way that she had, Jane had invited anyone she ran across, the final approximate numbers had startled her brother although he had said nothing.

And on the night, as they left their coats, both Christopher and Jane laughed together a little at the sight ahead of them. The whole of the first floor double sitting-room had had its furniture moved to the adjoining study, and the space that had been achieved seemed amusingly incongruous like a man without his wig.

Jane leant towards Archie confidingly, her mouth still open in exaggerated wonderment. 'I feel I'm in some marvellous Russian novel!'

'Oh Jane, I don't think so.'

Archie could never resist his sister's teasing. But looking around it could be seen that his reckless and clumsy venture into gaiety was amusing the other guests too and thus was achieving against all odds – a celebratory and carefree atmosphere within his Kensington flat.

Sometimes Laura tried to do without her friends. She would lie on her bed, listening to the answer machine pick up a message, usually just a commonplace reminder of a bill owing. She would use that moment of disappointment to examine – how did she feel with the disappearance of the friends of the sort that bestowed self worth? The sun still came through the bars of the basement window and the birds still sang outside; nothing apparently changed with failure. But some emotion was struggling through and very quickly emerged – it was liberation and she didn't trust it one bit. No. She preferred the drearily familiar, its sights set and its commonplace highs and lows. There, she knew where she was. And, anyway, this freedom was denied her, these friends wouldn't let her go; their calls always came, their invitations and chats and she was happy for it.

Angus alone of these friends had reverted to the scrupulous courtesy and brilliantly uninterested smiles of their first meeting. Tonight at this party, he was sitting over in the corner and he raised one hand in sharp greeting, turning at once to confide some quite unconnected piece of gossip to the boy at his feet. They were then obscured by the engaged pair, Christopher and Jane, who grinned and bowed away from the 'hoorays' thrown their way.

Looking across at them from behind the kitchen table, Laura felt a sharp rush of loss, peculiarly unjustifiable – since it was the loss of something unknown to her. The best defence she could come up with was 'old age' – their compensation for it.

Seeing her sitting in the kitchen, alone amongst the revellers there, Edward came over and crouched at her feet, then disentangled himself with a grunt of amused self-reproach at his aching bones, pulling a chair to sit beside her.

'Us old folk! How is Charles?'

'He's very ill.'

Edward froze, as timid as a deer surprised. 'I'd heard he was unwell – I'm so sorry.'

'I'm afraid it's only a matter of time.'

'Oh, my dear –'

He rose and beckoned to Penelope, who had waved to them from the other room. She came over and sat too; she and Laura talked about Charles. As they did so, a genuine feeling of loss permeated Penelope's conventional resignation; they spoke of his beloved dog and his fury at his own father's eccentricities. Though amused by Charles's father, Penelope understood that Hilary's insistence on convention, having created his own rules within that order, had dug deep into Charles's little protective veneer.

As she moved off, with a last regretful squeeze of Laura's arm, Edward said, 'Oh, I remember coming to lunch, wasn't it with Freddie? You must have only been about . . .'

He patted the air with mournful recollection.

'And a puppy I seem to remember – and oh you're right – Leadbelly! "Easy rider". Oh dear. What's his new place like?'

She didn't like to tell. Nature had not made its usual efforts in the surrounding land, but with perverse obstinacy, it was yet spurning outside help.

'It's nice!'

'Oh, but Kentigern – it was a place of God.'

Laura suddenly felt outraged and hurt at Edward's stubborn snobbery, the insistence on the past in the face of Charles's pathetic struggles – should he let go now that he had no remaining glory to hang on to?

'Not only God.'

She continued, describing the lead up to the incident on the beach, but as she reached the moment of the man's substituted erotic manipulations, her throat dried and closed up. Brushing that aside, she moved straight on to the strangling, that was clean.

'Oh my dear. Oh my dear.'

Seeing how upset he was, she relented, went on to tell him how she had at the time believed herself saved by Jesus – or perhaps, one of his local emissaries?

Catherine had come up, was listening and now joined in cautiously, 'So, did you actually see – Him?'

Certainly Laura had once thought she had, shyly slipping in an outlined saviour when drawing and playing in the months after it happened. But she had no wish to stamp that infantile, near-death dream into an authorised visitation by producing it now. The imagined sight had been as clear and as neat as a suburban dream, and its creation had all the puerile hallmarks of bourgeois justice – she had been picked to receive the grace of salvation, but the attacker himself? How about a bit of redemption going his way? But she hadn't told anyone about the incident at the time. If she had perhaps he would have been saved, and others too. To amuse, she altered her tone to one of certainty.

'Yes.'

'What did He look like?'

'Beard, robe, staff – the lot.'

Catherine laughed, Laura too.

'I'm sure I didn't – but if I had, it would have been that hackneyed no doubt.'

'God would appear in whatever guise was most soothing to a child's conception.'

Edward sounded genuinely distressed still, she had expected exultation and he went down in her estimation.

'Really, I don't know what to say – we wish them all the best!' Having been gathered into the main room for the host's speech, Laura watched Christopher sweep his bride to be into his arms in what she took to be a European gesture. It gave her a shiver of tender distaste – it seemed so admirably foreign.

Jane laughed and pushed him away – clapped her hands and drawled out the conventional sentiments of happiness and gratitude – trailing off with: 'Oh well . . .'

And at that familiar haughtiness everyone did laugh, Edward most of all. He had a child's erratic exuberance – intolerable or endearing, dependent on the mood or the prejudice of the observer.

But Laura had almost had enough of conviviality; she slipped out of the party. As she walked down the street, she felt that brooding excitement of loss, the end of a peculiar era. She only half-suspected the truth, that the one would drizzle into the next to render the difference indistinguishable – the drawback of sobriety's equanimity.

Chapter Thirty-eight

Charles had passed through the worst indignities of district nurses' kind public manipulations and now lay in bed immune to humiliation. Did he wish for that human stage back again? He spoke as if it were an effort, holding out Edward's gift for Laura to see.

'Quite a bit on Kentigern.'

In his new book, Edward had included a description of the walk that led unexpectedly to the ruined abbey, alluding again to the tale of its cave-dwelling saint, brought offerings of food by the local animals.

'Lovely.'

Laura looked at Charles, so often mention of the old place brought on melancholia and irritation. But he nodded, to say that she should continue reading. Remembering her manners, Laura held it up to Jeanette enquiringly – perhaps she wanted to take over?

Jeanette took it and looked at the place marked with Edward's covering letter of good wishes. 'But what did they bring him to eat? That's not quite explained!'

Laura understood Jeanette's need to be amusing, and tried to enter the fun.

'Berries?'

'Not quite the same as a proper meal!'

Jeanette turned to see that her sallies were appreciated, but Charles's face was dark.

People without charm (and how restful that is!) shouldn't attempt to make any stabs at it. She saw, as he had meant her to do, his displeasure, and handed the book back to Laura. She continued, reading aloud, as Charles lay absorbed in his irritation, 'It is easy to recreate an ancestral memory in this place, of the funeral procession from the sea shore; his followers walking in silence the two miles to this spot where the revelation had occurred. Now instead of wild boar, tame fallow deer watch whomsoever recreates this sacred pilgrimage, which cannot but move the traveller to thoughts of a religious nature.'

Chapter Thirty-nine

Laura sat beside her father's bed. She was a little stuck for what to say since she wasn't sure if he could hear her or not. She had the choice of platitude or profundity or truth. She picked up a pencil from the floor and twirled it. The dog had been chewing it.

She told him that she was attempting a poem about their fishing trip and Charles's features stirred in sudden anguish. She moved as if to rise – but then relaxed back down since his features remained the same.

He was using all his remaining energy to balance up there, any lapse in concentration and he would fall. She heard barking from down in the garden, and went to see what the terrier was doing, but he was out of sight. She looked back but her father wasn't reacting. She picked up the glass frog behind the curtains on the windowsill – she had given it to him in a burst of triumph having discovered it in a local shop aged ten – it was not now transformed into an object of beauty with the power of love. But what are considered ugly by many, children have a right to consider beautiful – and who's to say they're incorrect? According to the treatment centre's edicts, just as she could find herself touched rather than irritated by the necessities of design that would render these creatures unsuited for the epitaphs 'comely' 'beautiful' 'attractive', God should look on human shortcomings with similar fond indulgence.

And all the superstitious impulses – mankind's introspective broodings and conclusions – may be, like the black-lined camouflage running down its back, little design quirks necessary in the caves and swampy primeval forests, but here in modern civilisation? That's fine, let them stay anyway.

She put it back, next to an astronomy magazine that touched her again – his enthusiasm for the night sky. She ran her fingers over it, she had run out of things to say. She picked it up and lounged against the windowsill, as if to give his sightless presence the illusion of her ease.

His face remained contorted, abstractly so. For a second she thought he might be dead, since his eyes were open. But it came again, with ragged consistency, his next breath. She had always thought it strange – relieved of their lifelong duty, the eyelid muscles don't waste a second. At the moment of death they wash their hands of the whole of their life's work, they leave the eyes to stare up and dry up as they want. And it was a smug way to tell the quality of the thriller on screen ('strange . . .' leaning closer for a little aside to one particular date, trying to amuse him into sexual attraction, '. . . a noble death, his eyes peacefully closed' or words to that effect).

He was fighting to stay alive. A curious thing, since death was surely a return to that peaceful moment before all the fussing started, before life crawled up and over the god-damned planet. She flipped through to pictures of the Lagoon nebula, and the dust clouds within which new stars are forming – neither decorative (because unobserved) nor useful. She had occasionally reassured herself that there was nothing wrong with these discards, but again she felt the sickening jolt of uneasy possibilities slip into her mind. How can anyone think that in such a strangely designed universe, that God is at work? Some accidental positioning and sizing means our planet can sustain life. But out there and beyond, an eternity of black empty space and monumental dead planets turning for no reason round other suns, the equations of distance and mass dictating their pace. She put down the magazine.

The numbers might add up to a divine consistency, but it wasn't consistency that created life. Harmony produces a stale peace. Smash something and energy is released – if the whole make-up consists of broken and warped pieces, such appalling energy is released!

But Charles had liked peace and a place in which all creative movement had ceased. He was English and preferred the melancholy afternoon listlessness of the past – and what was wrong with that?

Few, of course, have any time for divinity, here in this practical world, but superstitious genes remain, uselessly flaring up from time to time, like appendixes. Certain conditions seem to trigger these reflexes (easy to understand in our animal natures). Returning to the house at dusk having mistimed the length of a walk. Graceful Benedictine ruins that glow with the unalterable gravity of history. And the men of genius, blessed by the gods, their vices not only forgiven but apparently encouraged – most people's reasonably constructed morality, whether taught or inherited, crumbling in their presence.

Usually, the hopeful human instinct for meaningful symbolism (in the more imaginative) will come to nothing and the realist will triumph. Corn circles can be explained, once the initial hopes have died down and coincidence is just that – the planet may spin, but each day the same odds return again. And intense reawakened memory that seems to urge the significance of return is merely the animal instinct for the familiar, to look for God in such, is as mistaken as a critic reading into a monkey's daubings, the emergence of an alarming new artist.

His mouth stayed open, gormless as a fish and, she supposed, with the same struggle for life.

Chapter Forty

From the dark church, Laura emerged arm in arm with Vivienne into the frosty air and the sweat from her ordeal froze her – it was a relief no longer to feel anticipatory terror. Standing as the coffin was lowered into the grave was quite a casual affair. Was the green grassy cloth a tactful touch to disguise the earth?

'I'm fine.'

She almost shrugged off Martin's touch – she knew that he too was reluctant to alter his professorial ways.

Now they could join the others, all of whom were beginning to allow themselves the relaxation of chat, previously curtailed in deference to the proceedings. As she moved from group to group, encouraging a return to the lightness her presence had momentarily suspended, Laura found herself shivering with some strange hangover of chemical nerves.

'Thank you – I know, he would! Where is Jeanette? I must see how she is . . .'

After Charles's death, Laura had received many letters. And she had found them surprisingly moving in their struggles to convey sincerity. Kielder had written with great brevity – he had had the grace not to suggest religious comfort. But at the end he asked if she might consider staying with them for Christopher's wedding – months off he knew, but . . . perhaps?

She had written back, and had accepted with pleasure – adding that she would indeed like to take advantage of their hospitality and bring a guest.

Now she saw Penelope, looking towards her with modest reluctance to intrude. Laura went over with polite eagerness.

'Thank you for your lovely letter.'

'Oh, my dear – of course! Edward was so sorry he couldn't be here.'

She took Laura's arm confidingly.

'But you're coming to stay for the wedding lunch? And with a *friend*? (Oh I hate that modern usage!)'

They laughed together.

'Yes.'

'I'm so glad, darling.'

Another letter she had been charmed to receive was from Alison, asking if she might be allowed to come to the funeral service? Laura remembered now, Alison had always rather liked Charles, certainly over Vivienne, had appreciated his giggles and capacity for easy enjoyment.

Now Laura saw her hovering and rushed to greet her.

'I didn't think you'd actually make it!'

They hugged each other. But after a while, it was tiresome having to keep up the sympathetic chat and the wonder at the reunion. Laura asked her in an undertone if she would like to escape later and visit Martin and Katie, staying in a hotel nearby?

'Yes! – Hello – Mrs Ruth!'

Mrs Ruth hugged Alison too, with brisk inattention. For a moment Laura felt annoyed by her madness that manifested now in excessive nostalgia, not for their solitary nights of television, but for the imaginary times of familial cosiness – Vivienne seeing her looking her way, came hurrying up and clasped her silently. At that, Mrs Ruth did start crying apologetically, and Vivienne too.

How pleased Vivienne must have been, here in this alien place, to gather reinforcements of past times, better times!

She held Mrs Ruth, who reiterated in a sudden quiet burst, 'He was mad to leave you.'

And with a pleasant little nodding jingle of whispered confidentiality, Vivienne said, 'I think so too.'

*

'Christ.'

Laura threw herself down on their bed, arms outstretched behind her head. Below them were just audible the subdued clinks of a country pub.

'If I'd stayed much longer, it might have been a double funeral.'

'What – you or her?'

'A triple funeral then.'

Ever since her marriage to Martin, and especially since her subsequent pregnancy, Katie found it easier to get on with Laura. Perhaps her maternal instincts were preparing for childish mood swings and inconsistencies, she had always found her funny and now she was restful too in her company. And Laura had stopped interpreting Katie's serene good nature as provoking stupidity, the sort that would disapprove of her type of cynicism. She went round to visit the two of them in their Clapham flat on a regular basis, found it restful to be able to turn on their television and sit in silence, eating Katie's rather delicious food without feeling the need to be charming.

Martin and Katie expressed thrill at her new romance, hinted at earlier, and at the manner of its initiation.

'A writing teacher – and is he a good poet?'

'No.'

'And do you mind that?'

'Not really.'

And she didn't. She could hardly say that it was really only the ease of this new relationship that gave her concern – since the whole point was that she did not feel that familiar all-consuming quest to beat the odds – and so did not feel concern at all. Laura had no idea what was natural anyway. She trawled through memories of literary love affairs, but she could think of so few writers who explored this particular avenue, she supposed that no obstacles at all was not a particularly promising theme.

But – she was longing to talk! The writing course having finished, she had sent Stephen the unfinished poem and he

209

had responded at once – how delightful! She had known he would, but how often had similarly instinctive certainties come to nothing?

'When did all this happen?'

'A couple of months ago.'

'A couple of *months*?'

'Well, it all seems to be going quite well.'

Alison alone seemed embarrassed by the subject, because she sat saying nothing. But she felt her own silence and asked awkwardly, 'Did you tell him it was for your father?'

'The poem? No.'

Laura knew that the 'for' aspect referred to a deficiency within it, but she admired Alison for her stance and didn't comment. Martin took up the funeral sheet again for another professionally psychological examination of Laura's created tribute.

'Verse one. Trumpet – a phallic symbol?'

'No.'

'Verse two. You feel your life has no meaning?'

'Not exactly.'

'Verse four. You find it easier to relate to men?'

'Of course!'

Chapter Forty-one

Laura introduced Stephen to Christopher in the early days of their friendship and Christopher had taken a liking to him. He got into the habit of ringing him. He liked his grave humour, considered it dignified. When Angus suggested to him that Stephen's poems hardly lived up to the high level of his demeanour, Christopher answered mildly by quoting one line that he liked, evidence that there was something there. Old age had not tempered Christopher's formidable will; Angus knew that his opinion was not going to be changed by presentation of fact.

They had drifted back into a friendship of sorts, and now Angus sat for him again, with his new social worker boyfriend Philip beside him. They had met at a party and Philip had done the entire running; he was a most delightful dynamo and it was considered by all that he was a considerable force for good in Angus's life. That he drank almost as much as Angus was ignored – he was young. Christopher liked his looks and his enthusiasm, once again he was swayed by the energy of youth. Tonight, Philip was busy, and the session was relaxing.

Later, they joined Laura and Stephen for dinner and Christopher made a big effort to cultivate this friendship further. He had so few new friends and these rare occasions still had the excitement of the chase. And Stephen laughed at his relentless desecration of old literary classics, his wheedling manner of insistence. He defended these particular favourites and, more robustly still, those lesser poets whom he considered needed his defence; he could be a little patronising. Angus and Laura listened in silence, but Laura smiled at Stephen encouragingly when his excited face turned to hers for her approval.

At one point, Christopher said again how much he had liked Charles. He described the night he saw him lose.

'Oh – his face – you see it was – *marvellous!*'

The prospect of marriage agreed with him. He must have been happy to have discovered and volunteered such conventional sympathy. Laura was touched.

After dinner, Christopher left to go back to work. As he left, he wound his arm round her waist in most insinuating fashion. But she had grown used to his ways and her affront could not be sustained. To keep poking the feeble flames of outrage would seem juvenile indeed.

Laura would have liked to have gone home too, but she indulged Stephen's wish that they stay with Angus for coffee, he so rarely showed such conviviality in the presence of her friends.

New to it, Stephen still liked to muse on Christopher's energy.

'– But consistency of vision for these prolonged periods takes a staggering strength of constitution.'

('Yes, a coffee, thank you.')

'Yes. I suppose anyone can have a flash of vision (though few seem to) but it's true that only a fraction can sustain that vision over the interminable time it takes to reproduce it.'

'And then the list is shortened further – some visions are really quite dreary.'

They left, and since it was too far to walk, they got the tube. Standing on the packed Circle Line train, they lowered their voices to discuss the evening, amused that they had to do so, surrounded by late-night revellers who had lost their daylight indifference, and who looked ready to listen with enmity to any hint of sobriety.

Laura liked being with Stephen; his silences were a relief. She had enough friends who chattered, God knows! But did she love him? The thought preoccupied her. She felt resentful in the middle of the night, lying beside him unable to sleep, knowing that the next day was now effectively ruined. If only she were alone! And the list of grievances would add up, perhaps she was not suited to a fucking relationship, its domestic demands and inconveniences. She would sigh loudly, almost a cry, and pull the blankets up fretfully. But he would turn and put his arms round her, still sleeping, still snoring, take her hand, return her squeeze, given in a moment of regret for her churlishness.

It seemed too placid for love. And spitefully she would think of the constrictions in her life, being with him. So how did it go? Oh I see – you meet someone, have a few dates, fuck (and thank God that's out of the way), see him the next week, the meetings grow more frequent – is this a relationship? (Oh she knew that it would, the very placidity in her soul told her that.) And after a few stumbling blocks – yes, he agrees – it is and they are together.

Conscious of her silence, Stephen leant towards her casually, holding and swinging the ceiling spring of the carriage like a toy.

'So will happiness produce another novel from Angus do you think?'

He liked to amuse himself with her views, produced with the slapdash indifference of a ruthless carpet seller. He would brace himself too for more dutiful questions whenever they arose; delicate emotions provoked by their relationship were not pushed aside. However, in this instance, much as she was prepared for her role as humorist, it was their stop and they got off.

Chapter Forty-two

Laura had wanted Stephen to accompany her to the Kielders' house, she wanted to introduce him to the subtle charms of the aristocracy. But he was busy and she hadn't liked to add to his mildly anguished regret. One of the reasons she liked him was for his lack of social curiosity. But then at the last moment, he had found himself free, and with a faint air of subdued triumph, had announced that he would be able to come along for one night – and for part of the wedding lunch the next day. She suspected that he had arranged this timetable alteration in order to be a support.

As they drove through the beeches lining the drive, he made no comment.

'Hello! Hello!'

Kielder stood on the steps to welcome them – a most unusual honour. It was customary for his days to be spent in front of his computer, now that his son had lured him into its complicated world.

('It's most intriguing – I tap away at it as timidly as a spinster – but I must say, it can't be resisted.')

'How *is* Tom?'

It had weighed on her, this subject. It certainly contained many hidden obstacles – but her chance had come and, indeed, Kielder seemed uninterested.

'He's marvellous – he's coming up next weekend I believe.'

'Give him my love.'

'Oh, I will! I will.'

That afternoon, she and Stephen went for a walk but she got somewhat lost in the myriad of brown paths and the one she chose took them away from the hills and alongside the woods. As they sheltered from the sudden rain under the poor protection of a beech tree, he laughed from under his coat and said, 'Country afternoons – all daffodils and melancholia!'

She liked that line too, it was more or less a quote from Angus's novel. But she felt it wasn't appropriate in this place, since she wanted him to like the countryside.

'Oh – now – everyone! Please – please! Here they are – the married couple!'

Christopher was torn – coming into the room, he wished to sidle away from the proclaiming Edward whom he had always despised. But still, he was happy and at the first notes of the wedding march put on loudly in the corner, he took a few jigging steps, waving his hands like a marionette. Edward was delighted – he left to find his camera.

Jane asked the room, 'I'm starving – when's our wedding feast – surely it must be soon?'

It wasn't so much that Christopher's eyes were irresistibly drawn in Jane's direction that indicated the extent of his love – after all, irritation can produce similar impulses. It was that when she turned to look back at him, his face responded like one of those daisies planted as children, unfurling gamely at the appearance of sun. And every utterance reflected this illumination, even when as mundane as the casual reply, 'I'm sure it must, but I haven't got a watch with me.'

It was a tribute to his enjoyment that Stephen put off his departure until the last train. In the drive they laughed together at one particular neighbour's wedding cake consumption – admirable! After she'd seen him off, Laura went back to join the party.

Edward came up to her and over the very loud music, shouted in a burst of confidence, 'Oh I do admire your delightful sweetheart!'

'Thanks!'

'I wish he could have stayed.'

'He had to get back – he's teaching tomorrow.'

215

It was a break in between songs and she saw Penelope smile at her tone of domesticity.

Edward's brother Archie was there and at one point she joined him on the sofa. Behind his head, on the writing desk, was the little antique metal golfing toy that she had denied herself the pleasure of using, the weekend of the address book theft. Now she pulled back the spring and allowed the club to whack the ball. She had to remind Archie of her name – he, perhaps because of his premature ageing, looked identical now to his younger self.

In an effort at compensation, he made a great deal of her trip the next day to visit the old place in memory of Charles.

'I think that's a marvellous idea!'

She understood that he was suppressing his normal dislike of sentimental gestures and in spite of the reasons behind this burst of kindness, she was touched.

Chapter Forty-three

In the mist, the distant trees were as tastefully grey and indistinct as any old-fashioned photograph, their short-comings hidden. By the time she had reached them, the sun had revealed their damp trunks and she felt happier. Soon she would reach the view that surely would produce some meaning. And there it was. She stood a while and then walked on.

She felt fond of the blackened statues of saints, exact copies of those on Prague's famous bridge. Not here one after the other in line as were their original counterparts, instead they were dotted randomly through the park, writhing on their plinths, brought to life by their twisting and grovelling garments. This one, standing with awful dignity, his folds hanging still, was grim with lifelessness, thus could be said to represent the timelessness of religion perhaps.

In the distance she could hear the diligent whine of the hedge-cutting machine. She had to pass the ruins; though it was mid-week, there were some visitors idly walking there too. She continued to the top ridge. From here the sea was visible, but even from this distance she could hear the faint happy shriek of families and she felt disinclined to join them. After a while, she judged it right to return. Wandering through the skeletal remains of the refectory she trembled with boredom and cold.

Walking away and into the park, she looked around. Although feeling exposed in all this space, she was now alone. Moving under the shelter of a large oak tree, she pulled out an envelope with a piece of paper inside. She thought she'd better read it aloud, checking again that no one was around.

To dad

I said
I like the word trumpet
It reminds me of an elephant
Or a daffodil
He said yes
And we carried on to the river in black and white

I feel exhausted from daytime dreams
And that I fill my life with silliness
Waking in the afternoon.
Although, God knows, that's fine
A child scraping away on the floor
Colouring in a picture

From across the river,
An unknown child would appear
Muffled up and eager to be of help
Soon to leave the safety and the comfort of being of use
Walking side by side,
Like two men, pals

Reading the finished poem in a coffee shop in St Christopher's Place, Stephen had laughed, it had been the involuntary laughter of rediscovered delight and she had been charmed. He had (in his cautious Scottish tones) encouraged her personal ceremony, though the doubt in his eye was flattering too. Perhaps he had thought the reading at the funeral service was enough – but he was not one to dwell on shortcomings.

She folded it up into enough of a ball that it could be buried and started digging at the earth with a stick. But the roots prevented any sort of access and the thought of one spatter of rain revealing it was embarrassing; this whole new age ceremony was very far from her natural inclinations. She spotted an animal hole and pushed it down that, then some more since the paper was still just visible. She thought of his dead face – drawn and contorted. What could she say about the comforts of religion? That space itself, would turn and make its way back and start again? She would have liked a full stop and a full stop was probably the case. And her near death here and unlikely salvation that had seemed to suggest so much? Just as Christopher had implied, it had meant nothing, just an accident – and surely that was a relief? No need to seek for links and hints of meaning. No need to feel the disappointment of not having lived up to some mythic promise.

Taking it out of her pocket, she pushed the green chocolate frog with its splayed black hands down the hole too. She had thought it a suitable offering, since some creature would be able to eat it.

Debating, she had asked Stephen in the shop, 'Do you think the silver foil is poisonous though?'

'Oh, no.'

But although well meaning, Stephen didn't know much about nature. And anyway, he had been contemplating the expensive Italian biscuits, and had been unable to prevent his fingers toying with their transparent boxes. Finally he had picked one up for the third time with a guilty pleasure, saying with a furtive look towards her, 'I think I will get these . . .'

Now this remembrance of his selfishness pleased her – and his lack of taste (they had looked repulsive) amused her still.

The sex was neither passionate nor frequent. She at first had found his hesitation strange, since she knew it came merely from a quite un-perverse lack of inclination. She knew he liked her and his liking was increasing; her indifference towards this side of things rendered their union quite easy and safe. She felt that too much emphasis was placed on sex anyway – it was an English tradition that life could get by quite well enough without it.

As she walked on, she thought about the burdens of a relationship and how to understand them. How much of his life should she take on? Oh it's all very well, the two being strong for each other, but on her own her life was simple because no one was around to witness it. If she was ill, she had no need to reassure anyone. If she had some furious time of self-doubt, she had no need to disguise it, but could just watch a video on her own till it passed. And if Stephen grew ill – if he found himself dying?

How much easier a solitary life of simple modern and lonely design was, than this romantic and magnificently crumbling set-up, that needed constant attention. She had no idea what the benefits of love were – she really didn't. She was curious, it was an interesting subject, if only she could ignore her guilt at the coldness of the question.

She looked back at the distant grey stones and the few appreciative lingerers, now ready to go home to their tea. She too thought about the hotel dinner coming with Martin.

It was three months since Charles's death and already she was thinking past his face to more interesting images.

'Your first visit?'

The lady behind the counter was kind looking, and there was no one else in the gift shop at that hour.

'I used to know it when I was a child.'

'Has it changed much?'

'Yes.'

The lady placed the eleven pence change down flat on the counter.

'I expect you have too.'

What had she meant? For some while this preoccupied Laura. She drove out of the turning, and as she twisted down the lanes, smiling to herself and replaying the incident, she realised that she had missed the main gates, that had signalled the start of holidays as a child. She reversed and finding them, stared through at the avenue.

She felt almost relieved that the whole place was a disappointment. The basics all were there of course still, but they had clipped, tidied and dictated the sort of behaviour expected on the notices at discreet distances from the tourist paths, warning against dogs off leads, walking on the lawns, not leaving rubbish – they had managed to sanitise all life away. It was the third most popular tourist destination in Northern England she had read, and they had won an award for their excellence.

She was tired of trying to encourage memory. It was hard work, silencing the entertaining chat that took up her thoughts. It seemed that placidity had at last replaced the overdone poetry of nostalgia. She started the car and drove on.

Chapter Forty-four

Perhaps it was because of the unusually long time they had spent in each other's company that day, walking round prospective cottages, joking and finding them hideous that the humour, by the fourth house, had worn off.

Laura felt weary and bored. Martin, seeing this, put too much into his reinvigorating high spirits, but having no luck, fell suddenly, as was his way in these circumstances, into a very distant efficiency. He spoke only to the estate agent, and then laughed falsely at her bad jokes in an intimate manner, guaranteed to exclude Laura. He thought that Laura would find the jokes and conversation tiresome and he was right.

They then drove from the estate agent's office to the station in silent gloom, hardly responding to the cab driver's local property price sympathies. The conclusion had to be that a great deal more looking was needed, and probably more money. Martin had thought that magnificent hidden treasures would be there, in the less prosperous North, just begging for his purchase. But instead had come the usual pokey rooms, and the photographed gardens that had seemed so charming, had in reality backed on to other houses, roads or chicken factory barns. He concluded somewhat wearily that his sights might have to be set further into the Scottish borders, where *surely* it would be cheaper?

But once on the train, they forgot their resentments for the first part of the journey at least. Passing through the northern countryside brought back hope and future prospects and the memory of their recent time in sodden surroundings were forgotten. They talked of past times, and this lapsed them back into the childish high spirits that Martin hadn't indulged in for some time; they re-enacted some peculiarly pedantic family incidents with the help of whatever railway buffet implements were to hand. This caused them considerable amusement and they were pleased to notice that the few other passengers in their carriage were also infected by their laughter, produced from the movements and dialogue back and forth between cutlery and cups. But then they began to find each other boring again, and each of them was irritated by the boredom they inspired and saw in the other. But rather than give way to this hostility, Laura followed Martin's example and leant up against the window so as to sleep.

When she woke up, she looked immediately at her watch in order to see to her satisfaction how much of the journey had been used up by what had seemed a long stretch. Only ten or perhaps twenty minutes had passed.

She asked with a yawn, 'How long have I been asleep?'

'Ten minutes. I don't know.'

They sat in silence through the stop at Grantham and on. It was dark now and the lights of some Midlands town looked as mysterious and alluring as an ancient port from the sea.

She thought of a dream she'd just had about a pig. At first she had found him embarrassing to be seen with, by his eagerness to be with her. For a start, he had been covered in dirt – how would it look? She had tricked him by suggesting he jump in the river for fun. He had rushed into the water and had had a real good time splashing around. Then they had walked further into the woods, him strolling along beside her, his feet scraping up leaves in a contented way, just chatting or not . . . just happy to be with her. As they walked on, she had realised that he would only credit her with good motives, would have no idea about her snootiness towards him, her snobbish social paranoia, or would just brush them aside without interest. He just thoroughly liked her and intended to stay with her – had no thought to do otherwise. And in spite of her snobbery (he was still not the most ideal friend) she had suddenly felt peaceful and happy.

223

'I've just had a dream about a pig who wanted to be my friend.'

She described it to him, and leaning back against the window he remarked, 'Obviously some sort of sex dream.'

Laura was sick of sex, and the whole matter of sex. If nowadays she was content to lie back chatting in the warm bed, not in some fiery union, unstable with the flames of bloody creation – so what.

'No, obviously some sort of spiritual dream.'

And the Indian man who was smoothing the safety instructions as he waited to get off at the next station, smiled at Laura and nodded, so she took that as a sign that he agreed with her.

Acknowledgements

Heartfelt thanks to

Jon Riley,
Brian Clarke and Garry Cooper.
Clare Conville and to all at Coville and Walsh.
To everyone at Faber and Faber, especially Lee Brackstone
and Helen Francis.